Rightfully Mine

Rightfully

Mine

by Aggie Villanueva

THOMAS NELSON PUBLISHERS
Nashville • Camden • New York

Published in Nashville, Tennessee, by Thomas Nelson, Inc. and distributed in Canada by Lawson Falle, Ltd., Cambridge, Ontario.

Printed in the United States of America.

Library of Congress Cataloging-in-Publication Data

Villanueva, Aggie.
Rightfully mine.

1. Rizpah (Biblical figure)—Fiction. I. Title.
PS3572.I35 1986 813'.54 86-747
ISBN 0-8407-3050-0 (pbk.)

Dedicated to Eddie,
my Caleb and
my Hanniel

Acknowledgments

Only a writer understands how important the help and support of others is in the long process of completing a book. I extend my sincere gratitude to:

My husband, Eddie, who endures the torment of living with a writer, possibly the most dreaded fate known to man. I want the whole world to know how thankful I am to have him.

My children, Eddie, Nicky, and Angie. Not only do they say they support me; they prove it by their interest and their willingness to give me the time to work.

Thomas A. Noton, whose love and inspiration has opened up a universe to me.

Jim Johnson, who fires me up to shoot for the stars, but be satisfied if I only hit the moon.

Deborah Lawrence, Charlotte Adelsperger, and Jill Blanche, whose encouragement has spurred me on.

And especially, my mother.

1

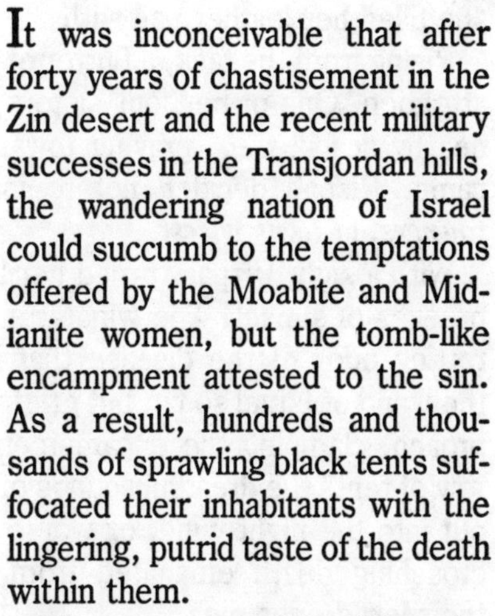

It was inconceivable that after forty years of chastisement in the Zin desert and the recent military successes in the Transjordan hills, the wandering nation of Israel could succumb to the temptations offered by the Moabite and Midianite women, but the tomb-like encampment attested to the sin. As a result, hundreds and thousands of sprawling black tents suffocated their inhabitants with the lingering, putrid taste of the death within them.

The vast camp of Israel lay crippled by plague. They huddled piteously beneath arcing acacia branches along the oasis-like stream of Abel Shittim, the only shelter available in the scorching summer sands of the Moab plains. Israel was halted only a few miles east of the Jordan they yearned to cross.

In the southwest corner of camp, among the tribe of Manasseh, Rizpah, the second-born of Zelophehad, grabbed a leather pail from a peg on the center pole of her family's tent. Unnoticed, she hurried from her father's crowded sickroom and headed for the nearly dry stream. Rizpah's brow crinkled in apprehensive muse as she made her way through camp. She shuddered as she filled her leather pail with the cool waters of the creek.

Rising from the task, a flutter of white garment caught her attention. One of her four sisters, Tirzah, stood beneath a nearby acacia tree, praying toward the tabernacle outside camp. Rizpah decided not to interrupt her. *Perhaps the youngest of us is wisest.*

With a sigh, Rizpah turned her face back into the eastern breezes of sunset. The wind attempted to dispel the dank, rotting odor of the disease that had claimed over twenty thousand of Israel so far, but grief and dread resisted the approach, clamping the encampment like a vise. From each row of tents the dreadful sounds of mourning were squeezed out into the night wind, or worse, the dreaded hush of encroaching death emanated from where families watched their loved ones die.

Lugging the water, Rizpah returned to where her family's tent squatted, enveloped in dreaded hush. The front and back tent flaps were stretched taut over wooden doorposts, desperately sucking in fresh air to alleviate the humidity caused by too many bodies, crushed inside the tent's confined receiving room.

Rizpah stole into the tent, praying for anonymity among the throng of neighbors murmuring their concern for Zelophehad to her sister, Hoglah, and her husband, Ludim. Zelophehad's nephews, whom he had treated like the sons he never had, milled about with awkward attempts to receive the guests. They and their wives were the only relatives present, as all Zelophehad's brothers (save two younger half brothers) had died during their desert wanderings. Blessing her cousins for their help with a silent benediction, Rizpah skirted the crowd.

She paused at Zelophehad's door to finger the goat hair partition, remembering. Last year she had mended the ragged edges of it for her father. In jest Zelophehad had claimed he couldn't sleep for the lamplight that crept through the torn edges of his door, from his giggling daughters' all-night festivities.

In truth, he had had trouble sleeping since Mamma died birthing her fifth daughter, fourteen years past. Now, *his* death was upon them, and the milestone would birth a life of uncertainty for Rizpah and her sisters, trying to survive without a man in a nation caught firm in racking labor pains itself. Forty years of desert wandering for a people impregnated with long-awaited promises, forced a violent labor that only now was beginning.

I mustn't be so morbid. Father will recover. Rizpah tried to relax her brow. At thirty-eight, her face bore few marks of aging, but her lightly tanned skin stretched tauter than usual over high cheeks and a square jaw, etching lines of strain around her thin mouth.

Her hair, tinted rich as mahogany bronzed from the lamplight, swung back hurriedly from her face, as if to avoid the candid gaze of her light brown eyes. Intelligence shone in those eyes, and a glimmer of ardent affection. The discovery of those lights in her eyes added intrigue to the interest shown her by cousin Hanniel, son of one of Father's deceased brothers and leader of their tribe of Manasseh. She hoped the interest would be subdued when he recognized that latent affection was not meant for him.

"How does my brother-in-law fare?" a voice shrilled beside Rizpah, startling her.

"Not well, I fear, Aunt Puah. He's sleeping now."

"It's such a shame," clucked Puah, wife of Zelophehad's oldest half brother. "I was telling Enosh, when your father first took ill...'It's a shame,' I said to him, 'that we have none of those learned Egyptian doctors here in the desert.' "

"We're doing all we can to make him comfortable," Rizpah mumbled, tugging at the doorflap as if to enter Zelophehad's room.

"I'm sure you are, my dear. I'm *sure* you are." Puah paused, but not long enough for Rizpah to escape.

"I can just feel the arrogance of the Moabites and Midianites as they sneer down at us from the eastern heights."

Puah squinted as if she were imagining the scene. "They shall forever be remembered as the country who could not match us in battle but defeated and immobilized us by their friendship—the friendship of their beautiful women, that is. Because of Israel's immorality and idolatry we stand thus, mourning in the tents of our loved ones." Puah looked back at Rizpah and clucked. "It is a shame that your father's good name will be smeared by his falling in *this* plague."

Rizpah glared at her aunt, dropping the partition to hiss, "Many men have fallen in this plague who are innocent of its cause, as they have also in the plagues of the other desert. How else could an entire generation die in only forty years? Or would you rather we tarry in the wilderness until they all die of old age? A few more seasons here, and you too will go to a sandy grave, denied your inheritance."

"I would think you could keep a more respectful tongue under the circumstances."

"If I were a man rebuking you, you would heed my words."

"When you are ready to bear the burdens assigned to men, I will give heed to you, but until the Lord Elohim changes the status of impertinent women I am still your elder and worthy of that respect." Puah jutted her chin haughtily.

She is right, Rizpah realized. *Why do I think anyone should give heed to me?* "Forgive me." Her shoulders drooped as she sighed. "I am weary. I only believe we shouldn't judge all the men who fall in the plague of Baal-Peor. That is the privilege of Ha-Elohim, the true God."

"Then I would assume it is also the privilege of Elohim, and not you, to judge my tongue." Puah had spoken sharply, but when she saw Rizpah's weary countenance and the dark circles under her eyes, her voice softened. She patted Rizpah's arm. "I meant no offense to Zelophehad. I came only to bring you and your sisters this bread." She held up a reed basket. "Let us keep peace at your father's deathbed."

Words of thanks formed on Rizpah's lips as she reached for the basket, but Puah's last word struck out at her and her arms fell limp at her side. "My father is not dying."

"But," the older woman sputtered, "you yourself said his generation must die before we can possess the land. Surely you realize it is time?"

Why don't you count off the number of years for me, my aunt? The press from the crowd of neighbors, mingled with the summer heat, added steam to Rizpah's anger. *Reason all you like. I will not let Father go!* she swore, clenching her fists but keeping her peace before Puah. Her aunt's hand fluttered on Rizpah's arm before she clucked again and strode away, shaking her head.

This plague. Curse this plague. It gives Aunt Puah an excuse to wag her tongue and threatens to steal my father. But my sisters and I will restore him to health. Rizpah threw aside the door flap.

The black goat-hair walls of Zelophehad's room offered little aid to the lamp's attempt to illuminate the cubicle. In rhythm with her sister Milcah's sobs, fingers of shadows streaked grotesque mirages of grief across the faces of those who lined the partitions.

Zelophehad slept fitfully on his woven reed mat in the center of the room, his hair and beard drenched with the sweat of fever and the stifling, trapped heat. At his head lay Mahlah, the oldest of his five daughters, an invalid who was propped against the thick fleeces she used for support in her chair. She wrung cloudy, tepid water from a rag to mop Zelophehad's brow.

Rizpah hurried to fill a bowl with fresh water and nearly tripped over Mahlah's lifeless legs. They lay at such an awkward angle Rizpah was sure she must be in pain. Reaching down, she tucked her sister's legs into a more comfortable position and was rewarded with a grateful smile.

Still, the motion threw her off balance, and she stumbled backward over Joshua, who was sitting cross-legged beside

Zelophehad's pallet. Joshua's friend, Caleb, reached out to steady her with a firm grasp. Her heart raced at the touch. *Why do I always behave like a fool in Caleb's presence?* she fumed, embarrassed at her bumbling; then she hung her head in shame. *Here am I, thinking of my own desires when Father is so ill.*

"Are you well?" The voice of Moses startled her as he burst into the room with his usual vivacity. His sharp eyes squinted at her pale features, and he repeated, "Daughter of Zelophehad, are you well?" Rizpah struggled to overcome the start Moses had given her. She wanted to say, "I am not the one in need of your concern," or anything that would channel the focus of everyone's attention away from her, but she could only stammer.

"Noah." Zelophehad's breath expelled a raspy whisper.

Thankful for the interruption, Rizpah bent to him and covered his hand with hers. She wondered that he called her *Noah*, her given name, and not the nickname he had pegged her with so long ago. He said the name *Rizpah* was more befitting one who could bake bread on the heat of her anger.

"Noah," her father breathed slowly and with obvious difficulty. "Is everyone here?"

"Everyone?"

"Are my half brothers here?"

"No, Father."

"I thought not."

"But my cousins are all here. The sons of your dead brothers are a great comfort to us."

"Hamiel also?"

Rizpah didn't answer, only patted her father's hand.

Zelophehad's eyes fluttered. "Bring my daughters and my half brothers. I want all my family here—to bless them." His eyes succeeded in opening, and as Rizpah looked into them she admitted at last he was truly near death.

Moses and Joshua and Caleb, Israel's ennobled leaders, rose tactfully to leave, but Zelophehad reached a trembling arm toward them. "Please stay. I said I want *all* my family present." Moses' eyes softened, and the three men turned back to face the old man's bed.

"Bring your cousin Ludim, Hoglah's husband, and Tirzah's betrothed, cousin Reuben, also," Zelophehad whispered to Rizpah. His eyes were closed again, but she nodded and left.

The group that quickly assembled around Zelophehad's pallet was solemn. Oppressed by the stagnant heat, they waited, increasingly aware of the smothering presence of the death angel.

The old man's head was propped on folded blankets. Although even his snow-white hair and beard seemed ashen gray, he seemed to have gained some strength. His eyes were open and alert, ready to perform the final act of the head of a household: the prophetic blessing.

"Moses—you who are like a brother to me," Zelophehad wheezed. Moses came closer. "We are the last, aren't we, my friend?"

"The last of our generation, yes." Moses nodded and started to speak again.

"No," Zelophehad inhaled sharply. "Do not pity me. We both know the mercy of Elohim Hayyim, the living God, do we not? So we must accept also His judgments. He is the object of all our human striving, and the end to all seeking. I look gladly to the end." He coughed weakly but his voice gained volume. "What will you do when this plague is over?"

Moses sighed, and his white head shook from side to side. "Israel deserves to be left here at the mercy of the surrounding hostile lands. This new generation is no more faithful than ours."

"Come, you old, wandering Aramean, we both know you won't abandon them. Elohim's mercy and wrath must be learned anew by each generation, and you will stay to teach this one."

Moses looked at the tenderness in his old friend's eyes

and smiled in agreement. "I will remind them of Yahweh's goodness to us." Moses used the name for God that Elohim Himself had spoken, and none but their leader dared breathe. "I will make them ashamed for their rebellion and call them to repentance. Then they will be prepared to enter the promised land."

The dying man's face was paler, but his voice was steady. "There is now not much distance between the desert and the sown. The people will be hard pressed to wait until Elohim sends them to battle for Canaan."

"I will hold them in rein."

"I know you will, my friend. May your strength be firm."

"And yours." Moses' voice was husky.

Zelophehad offered thanks for Moses' friendship as the men gripped arms.

"Where is Joshua?"

"I am here, sir." Joshua came to Zelophehad's side.

"And Caleb?"

"Here, sir."

"Joshua and Caleb, I love you as if you were of my own tribe. All of Israel knows how you two led us to victory over the Amorite king, Sihon, and Og, king of Bashan, in the hills east of the Jordan toward the sunrise."

Zelophehad reached out and touched first Joshua and then Caleb's head. "May Ha-Elohim, the true God, always lead you in His victorious path." Joshua stepped back but Zelophehad took hold of Caleb's shoulder. "My friend," his voice was beseeching. "I am leaving my family without the protection of a man. They have no one on whom they can rely."

Rizpah's uncle Salu shuffled his feet and she saw him exchange resentful glances with her uncle Enosh. Her father kept his gaze intent upon Caleb. "Though you are not of our tribe, be to my daughters as a father and an uncle and a brother, as long as they need you." The pronouncement became a plea. Rizpah flinched at the thought. Caleb had always been her lover in her dreams.

Caleb placed his hand upon Zelophehad's thigh in the gesture of taking an oath. "I will do as you bid."

"Enosh and Salu, sons of my father but not my mother, come forward."

The men shuffled to their half brother's bed.

"Had my mother lived, you and Salu would not have, but because you were born to Father's second wife, after my brothers and I were grown, you are allowed to possess the promised land." Zelophehad's eyes wandered. "That is the only reason I ever had to question the wisdom of Elohim."

Rizpah's uncles reddened, their eyes bulging in anger. Zelophehad returned his gaze to them. "Enosh, if the wicked beckon you to ambush the innocent without cause, keep your feet from their path. Do not walk with them, Enosh.

"Salu, my youngest brother, you are as a ravenous wolf, but you will find it useless to spread the net for the righteous. You will become caught in the snare yourself." Salu's face purpled with anger, accentuating the yellowish bags beneath his eyes. He nodded, the jerky movement slinging sweat from his scraggly beard.

Zelophehad closed his eyes as if to blot out all thought of his brothers. "I would bless my daughters." His eyes opened and swept over the five of them. "How you all bear the mark of your mother's beauty, each with a different shade of her hair."

Mahlah, still by her father's side, slipped her hand quietly into his. Her firm chin showed none of the slackness of indolence or indulgence, while the lines of age that marked most forty-year-old women were only just forming around her brown, wide-set eyes. Her thin nose graced her countenance with a long, noble sweep, turning up at the end in pride, not impudence. Wisps of light brown hair swept in soft, natural waves around her face, highlighted by strands of a lighter almond-shell shade. Her eyes filled humbly with tears as she heard her father's blessing.

"Mahlah, my eldest, you were born the year Israel's military might was crippled by fear and we were sentenced to a bitter forty-year march in the wilderness. Perhaps that was a curse for you, but despite your lameness you were our first blessing.

"If your mother had possessed the strength of the healthy, your infirmity would not have distressed her so. Yet, even in your sickness, or perhaps because of it, you have strengthened us. Your weak frame possesses the powerful strength of love." Zelophehad's tone became intimate. "This is the strength of a mother of Israel. Though you will never know physical motherhood, all who know you shall inherit a portion of your love."

Mahlah released her father's hands to wipe the silent wash of tears from her face.

"Come, Hoglah, my daughter who is like unto a desert partridge."

Everyone shot questioning glances at Rizpah, as if she could explain why Zelophehad had skipped her in the order of blessing.

Perhaps this is to be my punishment. Rizpah berated herself soundly, recalling all the times her temper had flared and her stubbornness had caused conflict. *Surely I deserve a rebuke. I will never acquire the meek spirit of my sisters. But is that just cause to lose my place as second-born?*

The room was frozen by disgrace and uncertainty. Thirty-two-year-old Hoglah, the only married sister, stood beside her husband, her deep-set eyes searching his for direction in this awkward situation. Finding none, her broad nose quivered and she turned to Zelophehad. "Yes, Father?" Her wide mouth pursed with tension, and absently she stuck a crop of straight, straw-colored hair into the tight knot from whence it had escaped.

"Come to me," he said. Still Hoglah hesitated. Confused, she glanced at Rizpah, who shrugged her own bafflement, then sat before Zelophehad. He laid his hand lightly upon her shoulder.

"The desert partridge rarely soars in the clear, bright sky.

The heights seem to frighten it. If forced, it will take flight, only to drop into the next available cover. So you, Hoglah, have spurned dreams that soar beyond your reach, but do not spurn hope.

"As the partridge darts from rock to rock, so you dash from each completed task to stolidly face the next. May your children also drink from your well of duty and dig cisterns of their own to preserve for their children and their children's children."

Hoglah embraced her father and retreated to cousin Ludim's side. She pretended to shoo a gnat rather than admit wiping away a tear. Milcah, the fourth-born, did not await her father's call but sank to his pallet.

Milcah's topaz-hued hair swirled about her face with the tentative probing of sunlight constrained by dabs of drifting clouds. It crowned her high, regal forehead, lending a misty softness to the sharp lines of her nose and chin so like her father's. The creamy complexion of a youth of twenty winters smoothed her every feature and silhouetted dark, fawn-like eyes, set wide and hopeful, but now reddened with weeping. She waited for her father to begin.

"You were born twelve years after Hoglah. Your mother and I were sure she could bear no more children. When you came we drank greedily of the blessing. I suppose one could say we spoiled you, as much as is possible in the barren desert. There are not many opportunities to indulge a child here. Still, we took advantage of every chance to free you to enjoy childhood, and you have grown to expect more from life than we dared."

Zelophehad spread his fingers over the crown of her head. "Milcah, lovely queen who reigns over our hearts and the hearts of the young men of Israel, your beauty shines brightly; but there is no great strength in beauty. There will come a day when you will despise beauty, so be strong in faith."

Realizing that he was finished, Milcah smoothed her hair,

bestowed a smile of incomprehension on her father through a veil of fresh tears, and retreated.

"Where is my maiden of gladness?" There was an urgency in Zelophehad's voice, as if time was running out. Tirzah approached his bed from the opposite side. Her petite form squatted easily beside him, in contrast to the statuesque frames of her older sisters. Zelophehad gazed fondly at his fourteen-year-old daughter.

Even the greasy lamplight picked out the iridescent, silvery highlights in her dark honeycomb hair. It was straight like Hoglah's, but the effect was softer as it caressed her young face. Even in her grief Tirzah's cheeks bubbled in a crinkly-eyed grin for her *abba*.

"We knew when you were yet in your mother's womb that you would be our last reward from God, and we knew your mother would not survive. Our generation has lived in the shadow of death, always conscious that we would not share in the promised future of our seed. Tirzah, the oil of pleasantness to my old bones, though you are a maiden of only fourteen years, your youth is not a disgrace, as it is in many."

Rizpah flinched at what she feared was an implication aimed at her.

"Goodness is a crown to your head. You will be counted blessed among the daughters of the tribe of Manasseh and a treasure in the house of your betrothed. Because of you, Reuben's home will be a fortress of joy in the land the Lord has promised."

Reuben reached down to his beloved Tirzah. She rose and clung, weeping, to the chest of her betrothed.

Rizpah felt conspicuous. She stood clenching her long, slender fingers, all eyes on her. Her mature beauty was unscathed by the tension.

"Noah!" Zelophehad's voice sliced the air like a dagger, calling out her given name. Rizpah stole a glance at Caleb, regretting he must witness her disgrace. *He will never con-*

sider taking me for his wife now. She knelt beside her father with lowered head. Trembling, she awaited the dreaded rebuke.

"Noah, your mother named you for the rest and comfort you would bring her in caring for her invalid first-born, and indeed you were her salvation. Yet I must confess, you have not given your poor old father much rest. I have wearied myself seeking the wisdom to guide you rightly."

His voice was tender, but Rizpah's head hung further. She grasped his outstretched arm and sobbed, "I have failed you, Father."

Zelophehad took her hands. "No, my daughter," he sighed. "I fear I have failed you. My heart has rejoiced in you, but I have not the wisdom necessary to give you what you will need. Do you know why I did not bless you in the usual order of oldest to youngest?"

Everyone seemed to lean forward. Rizpah raised her head slightly as she shook it, but she still could not bear to look at him.

"You thought you were removed from your place as second-born, didn't you?" Zelophehad asked. "Oh no, my precious Rizpah." He reverted to his fond nickname for her. "You have always been quick-tempered, but that is not cause to disown you. I also know your faithful spirit. You have an undergirding of wisdom that bends your will."

Does he mock me? Rizpah wondered, and her head drooped once more, for she felt the most foolish of Israel's daughters.

"How can I make you understand your blessing?" Zelophehad paused. "As a people, Elohim chose us for His possession, and He made a covenant with Abraham. When I speak of these things, you think of the circumcision, but our covenant is not just of flesh. Circumcision was only the first step of becoming God's possession.

"Our desert wandering was another step. There will be many more steps in this journey to become His possession.

Some of them have been hard to bear, many that come will be harder still. This people has been chosen to show right to a world of wrong. Our covenant is with the God of love and mercy, but most of all, He is justice."

Zelophehad looked intently at her. "I have blessed you in this unusual manner, for you are unusual among women. You will stand for justice, and justice will circumcise you."

Rizpah shuddered. Was this a blessing or a riddle?

"Do you understand now the frustration of an old man? You have need of much wisdom, and I will no longer be here to guide you. Do you know how a father *needs* to feel he has prepared his children?" Impassioned, Zelophehad shook her shoulder. His eyes slid to where Caleb stood behind Rizpah, and they shone with the glimmer of an idea.

"I never understood your choice not to marry your cousin Hanniel. He is the leader of our tribe of Manasseh and eldest son of my eldest brother. For twenty years he has sought you for his wife."

Rizpah stared, perplexed at the abrupt change of ideas. She thought this issue had been settled long ago. Father became more puzzling by the minute.

"You didn't know that he proposed yet again when he knew I was taken by plague. Are you certain you could find no happiness with him?"

Rizpah looked bewildered but offered no answer. Zelophehad went on.

"I have never believed your claim of allegiance to the care of Mahlah as an excuse not to marry Hanniel. It was not until I discovered that your love for Caleb forced your choice that I understood...."

Rizpah heard no more. Her burnt amber eyes flashed an opalescent inferno. *How can Father say these things before everyone, especially Caleb? How does he* know? *Not even Mahlah knows. What must Caleb think of me now?* She could feel his questioning gaze burn her back.

In mortification she prayed that the earth would open up

and swallow her as it had Korah and his followers. Would that she had rebelled with them, so she would have already been swallowed—anything rather than face Caleb. Her hands opened and closed in painful fists, unconsciously. Her features contorted from the pressure of the questions she wanted to scream. *Why, Father? Why are you doing this to me? I must suffer this mysterious blessing—now why must you add this agony also to your death? Why?*

"I know you are distraught that I have uncovered your secret before all." Her father's steady voice broke through her thoughts. "It is my last gesture of fatherhood, Rizpah. Perhaps by this I can prepare you to bear the covenant.

"Let this, then, begin your journey. You think you will not survive, but your journey only begins this night. Stand firm, and do not run. Do not turn to the side. If you endure to the end, you will inherit the justice of the covenant."

Zelophehad slumped, breathless. "Leave me now." He raised his hand in an attempt to wave them all away but could not complete the gesture. "It is done...."

2

Rizpah stumbled out of the tent into the night, not caring where she would go, only gathering the skirt of her tunic to make haste.

Plunging through the rows of tents heading west toward the camp's edge on the Jordan's side, she dodged skilfully the many obstacles impeding her way. On the right loomed tentpoles obscured by darkness; on the left, buckets of diseased excrement awaiting disposal. Directly in her path a widow lamented her loss, a circle of moonlight bathing her rocking, solitary form. Rizpah swerved, ducked, and hurdled, picking up speed until she achieved a fast trot, to emerge at last at the vast camp's edge.

Gulping the cool night air, she attempted to calm herself. Her fists clenched her skirt convulsively. Facing the Jordan, her rigid back aligned against the graveyard camp that continued, unsated, to consume its dead, marking the hours till it could vomit up the body of her father also. She wished she could eliminate her problem with Caleb as easily as vomiting. She held her cramping midsection as if the humiliating bile would burst forth at any time.

Rizpah was aware of his presence even before she heard the scrape of thong against pebble. *What is he doing here?* The din of surging blood roared in her ears; yet she could hear the sound of Caleb's slow, even breathing behind her.

"The night is pleasant in Shittim under the starlit skies of the Moab plains," he said softly.

"Plains?" Rizpah scoffed. "A plain has meadows of waving wild grasses, with lilies of the fields scattered about." She seared the shadowed western horizon with her stare.

Such a plain could not be further from this barren desert east of the Jordan rift valley. The Jordan here was known as the Ghor, and it was but a trench incised in the distance. The moon was full, and the bright stars illuminated the inauspicious landscape—a perfect accommodation for the plague of Baal-Peor.

Along the Ghor to the north, Rizpah traced the distant blur of dense, jungle-like vegetation that ended too abruptly on the river. There steep, bare cliffs marked the foreboding entrance to the Salt Sea region in the south. Behind them in the east soared the mocking Moab mountains, and across the Ghor before her the promised land of Canaan beckoned. The possession of a peaceful land flowing with milk and honey seemed a millenium away from tonight.

"This plain doesn't have that," Caleb said.

"What?"

"This plain is not a meadow ripe with grass and bloom. It is a barren pit. But it *is* a plain."

"Would that be some of the wisdom you are so acclaimed for?" Immediately Rizpah bit her lip in remorse. "I am sorry. There is no reason to lash you with my tongue. I cannot fault you because my father—"

"I am sorry for making light of the situation," Caleb interrupted. "I only hoped to put you at ease."

Rizpah's back stiffened toward him. "Thank you, my lord. I would beg your leave now."

She moved aside to return to the tent, but her father's

blessing loomed before her like a barricade. *Your journey begins this night. Stand firm, and do not run. Do not turn to the side.*

She halted, her back still to Caleb. She was running. She had run here, and now she was running back to camp. Where would she go next? *Father is right. Turning aside will solve nothing. But how can I face Caleb? He knows. He knows I love him.* Rizpah nearly moaned aloud, but she knew she must face him. *Even if he thinks me as brazen as the Midianite women.*

With willful determination she turned to Caleb, and her breath caught at the sight of him so close to her. The moonlight turned the gray at his temples silver, and she could see his steady pulse beating silently. His striped summer tunic was sleeveless, revealing tanned, muscular biceps and sunburned forearms, and the neckline plunged deeply enough to allow dark, curly hairs to climb out. His broad chest heaved with each patient breath.

Rizpah had to tilt her head back to a dizzying degree to look him in the eye. For the first time their eyes met, and her head spun with exhilaration, even under the degrading circumstances. She could not tear her gaze from him. He shifted uncomfortably on athletic legs that attested to the restrained strength of tightly wound coils.

The man could not have seen seventy-nine years, Rizpah thought in amazement. "Why did you—" Her voice cracked and she tried again. "Why did you come out here?"

"I wanted to let you know I didn't take seriously the words your father spoke. He is sick unto death. A man can say many things on his deathbed."

There it was: her way out. She could laugh about it with Caleb. They would forget the whole episode, and maybe someday he would learn to love her. *Do not turn to the side. Stand firm and do not run.* She sighed.

"It would be so easy to let you believe that, Caleb, but it would haunt me. My father spoke the truth." Rizpah finished quickly and looked down. She could smell his sweat. Now that she was so close, would she lose him?

There was silence, then Caleb cleared his throat. There was more silence. Rizpah thought she would faint.

"But, I am an old man of seventy-nine," he finally managed.

Rizpah lifted her eyes to stare at him. "And I am a shy young maiden at thirty-eight."

Caleb conceded her point with a nod. *At least he is no idle flatterer,* Rizpah thought, a little disappointed that he had not assured her of her youthful appearance. There seemed to be nothing more to say. They stood close together for an awkward eternity, not looking at one another.

"I don't know what to... this has never... I am just an old widower."

Rizpah nodded. "And your daughter has decided not to wed until after the land is possessed, so that she should not become a war widow at eighteen years. There is nothing I don't know about you."

Caleb's eyes darted to her in surprise. She took a deep breath. "I suppose I should tell you everything. This night seems determined to strip me, to lay me bare to the world." Rizpah looked up into the blackness as if she hated it. "I suppose I have nothing but to submit. You will think me unforgivably brazen, but you may as well know all."

Caleb kept his gaze upon the distant Ghor. Neither dared move. The wind whistled around them, as if laughing at their feeble attempts to carry on this macabre conversation.

"I hated your wife!" Rizpah's voice split the stillness. She glanced at Caleb, but his only reaction was to blink. *How can I be saying these things to him?* She wanted desperately to know what was going on behind those huge, thickly lashed eyes.

"Oh, it wasn't real hatred. It was childish jealousy. She had you and I wanted you. My father thought it was just the usual hero worship afforded you by the children of Israel," Rizpah snorted, "but it was more."

She resigned herself to letting the words spill out unchecked. "I remember you invited my family to sup with you and your wife. I was at the marrying age. In fact, I had just convinced Father to turn down cousin Hanniel's first proposal.

"It happened after the meal, when my mother and your wife—I could never bring myself to call her by name—were clearing away the bowls. You reached out and touched her hand. You complimented her, saying, 'We have eaten of only water and manna for these many years, but you somehow manage to make it delectable.' The spark that passed between your eyes was the same tenderness my parents shared, but far from touching me, it tore me asunder. I swore never to be near you again if your wife was present."

There was no bitterness in Rizpah's voice, only a toneless resignation to at last letting the truth be known. Releasing the hidden emotions of a lifetime was almost pleasurable. *But will he return my love?* Her temples pulsated in suspense.

"I am sorry I abided by that adolescent oath." She clasped her hands together and nearly brushed the front of Caleb's tunic with them. "She must have been a remarkable woman."

Caleb nodded stiffly.

Dear God of Israel, what must he think of me? Have I waited all these years only to chase him away with my babbling?

Caleb cleared his throat. "Is it true what Zelophehad said? Is this why you have turned down all of Hanniel's proposals?"

This was the hardest to admit. She nodded her head slowly. *Oh, why did I not keep silent?* She heard Caleb let his breath out, as if he had been holding it in anticipation of her answer.

Rizpah waited. It was all up to Caleb now. She had emptied herself before him. She felt as if she were writhing before him, frighteningly vulnerable to his tread. Caleb shuffled his feet and cleared his throat again. She wanted to slap him on the back to clear what seemed to block his voice.

"I am grateful for your honesty." His voice betrayed no emotion.

"It would not be fair to withhold this information from you after my father's speech tonight." Her tone came out too clipped in the effort not to sound pleading. Caleb finally looked at her again.

Rizpah met his gaze. They stood motionless, facing each other. *Throw your arms around me,* she wanted to scream at him. *Tell me you have admired me from afar and this is an answer to your prayers. Say you want to marry me at dawn. Say you despise me for the things I've said. Rebuke me for my immodesty. Anything. Just give me some response!*

"I beg forgiveness for this intrusion." Rizpah's uncle Salu tried to soften his words in reverence but his voice only took on a sinister quality. "Your father, my brother, has just been gathered to his people."

A thud echoed in the wailing night wind as Rizpah sank to weep among the thorns and rocks.

3

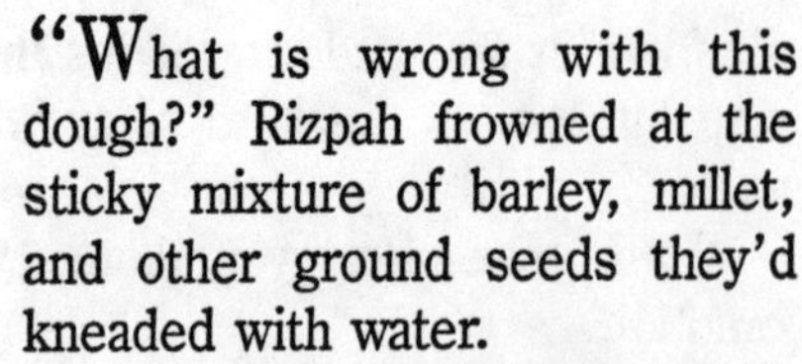

"What is wrong with this dough?" Rizpah frowned at the sticky mixture of barley, millet, and other ground seeds they'd kneaded with water.

"I don't know." Mahlah furrowed her brow, beating the dough. "It wasn't like this when I made bread before."

Having shaped the goop into what hardly resembled a wafer, Rizpah slapped it against the outside of the heated earthenware jar that served as an oven. "Oy!" Pointing at the bread that quickly blackened and cracked, she made a face and scraped the brittle cake from the oven's surface. Baking bread was still a new experience for the women of Israel who were born and raised on manna.

Tirzah interrupted her humming, which had been constant since yesterday when Reuben announced they would marry before Israel marched on Canaan this spring. "You forgot the oil." She pointed and elbowed Milcah, who laughed with her.

"The oil." Mahlah slapped her forehead with the heel of her hand and reached for a jar of olive oil, a trophy of their plunder from the wars against the Amorites. She smiled at Rizpah, but her laugh faltered when Rizpah didn't respond. The quick smile that once played at Rizpah's mouth had long been a stranger.

Rizpah knew how worried Mahlah was about her. How often in the nine months since Father's death had she scolded herself for the mounting alarm she caused in her sister's eyes—to no avail. She would rather take the plague than cause pain to Mahlah, but still the deadness of her soul increased.

The days of mourning were long past for everyone but her. Rizpah felt herself hurtling ever faster into the depths of a region familiar to her since earliest childhood, only then she wasn't falling, she simply abided there. Only since Father's death had she recognized her life's abode as a state of living death, and then her descent began with such dizzying speed she expected at any moment to . . . Expected? Yes, *expected*. Rizpah tasted the foreign word. Expectation could not exist in her living death.

Yet, in a flash, she knew with certainty this expectation was what bade her pitch tent in the region in the beginning, always awaiting. The events of the fateful night of Zelophehad's death began the pivotal period that would reckon whether Rizpah would be freed from this spectral region of unfulfilled expectations, or the tent pegs of her heart would be forever secured in its cold ground, without Caleb.

"Peace to you." Aunt Puah ducked into the tent, dripping with the latter rains of winter.

Mahlah, finished with the batter, wiped her hands and greeted their aunt, while a pensive Rizpah patted out barley cakes, remedied with the missing ingredient. She licked a tapered forefinger and tested the outside of the jar to see if its hiss was sufficient to brown the cakes properly this time. Milcah ladled cuts of cheese from the leather pouch the goat's milk had curdled in, enjoying the produce of her beloved flock nearly as much as she did caring for them.

"Aren't you the industrious little family?" A swift smile attempted to soften their aunt's features. She wiped raindrops from her face and shook out her shawl. "I can see you are all overcoming your grief."

The four sisters flinched. Tirzah's humming stopped.

"Really, Aunt Puah, I hardly think—"

"How right you are, dear." Puah interrupted Rizpah's instinctive protection of her sisters. "Forgive your crude old aunt, but I would think nine months is sufficient time to mourn." She peered purposefully at Rizpah. "I know it was easier for your sister Hoglah's grief to subside. She has her own family, and the four of you are alone—except, of course, you, Tirzah. I hear you and Reuben are cutting short your betrothal period."

Tirzah's eyes crinkled in pleasure. "Oh yes, Aunt. We will wed before he goes to war."

"May you be blessed with many sons." Puah scoured the room as if in search of something. "Enosh has told me the war census is nearly complete—and it is about time. Nine months since the plague, and now spring is upon us. The campaigns against Canaan cannot begin until Moses has recorded each man of age to fight. Now we have only to wait for Moses to..." Puah stopped short and sputtered. "Of course I don't mean I want him to...he has been a mighty leader of our nation and I wish him long life, but we all know that God has said...Oh dear, you know I don't mean to..."

Long-buried emotions stirred in Rizpah as she found amusement in her aunt's plight, but Tirzah took her usual pity on Puah. "We know you meant no disrespect, Aunt."

"Well, of course I didn't." Puah's hand fluttered against her chest. "I only wanted to give you the news about the census." She paused, then covering her head with her shawl, scurried out.

"A visit from our aunt is as entertaining as the caravan dancers."

"Rizpah!" Mahlah rebuked, but her face showed relief as she covered a smile with her hand.

Rizpah leaned forward, a wry smile curving her thin lips.

"Did you notice she knew of Tirzah's wedding plans? Reuben told *us* only yesterday. She is as one who puts a secret in a sling."

"Hush, now." Mahlah coughed to disguise a twitter and the two younger girls' mouths twitched with mirth. "We must respect our elders."

Mahlah's eyes wandered over Rizpah's features as if to plead for the animation of this brief reprieve to remain. Rizpah's heart rose to reward her sister's hope. "Ah, but you speak true when you say *elder.*" She forced a wide smile for Mahlah's sake.

This time her two younger sisters laughed outright. Mahlah clapped her hands. "All right. I think we should say the first blessing and eat, before I faint."

The bread finished, Rizpah plumped the cushions behind Mahlah and handed her the warmest wafer. Mahlah caught Rizpah's hand before she turned away. "Sister, my heart is full to see a smile again occupy your lips."

Rizpah looked deep into Mahlah's eyes and pondered just who cared for whom in their relationship.

"But it is not only Father's death that has stolen your joy, is it?"

So her forced smile had not fooled Mahlah. Rizpah shook her head.

"Caleb?"

Rizpah studied their clasped hands. How could she relay the agony—Caleb's rejection after her brazen confession; the heartbreak of a lifelong dream, shattered?

Mahlah patted Rizpah's hands. "Perhaps a little more time and the smile will lodge again on your lips."

"Until this war census, I wondered if Moses would hold us here in the plains of Moab, instructing us for another forty years," smirked an elder who plopped the last bag of stones marked with his clan's standard on the table before Hanniel.

"Do not be overanxious. He's not finished teaching yet." Hanniel winked, and his hoarse voice sounded as if it resisted the effort to speak above a whisper. Damp, russet waves of hair dangled beneath his striped linen turban as he bent to open the leather bag. The curtains of heaven were drawn, and winter's latter rains pelted the roof of the Tent of Meeting like unrelenting drums, striking the ground outside with such force that the torrents backsplashed waisthigh.

"With the plague ten months past, and the census nearly complete, we can finally begin battle plans." The excited elder continued, "The news of Moses' making double use of the census means he is looking to when we settle in the land."

The reference to Moses' dividing Canaan according to the names on the war census drew a frown from Hanniel. He shifted his stocky legs beneath the wooden table where he'd sat for an indeterminate period, recording the men of fighting age in his tribe of Manasseh. His left pupil gravitated inward, giving him the slightly cross-eyed look he took on when reflective. Rather than being offensive, the quirk marked him with the mischievous air of a little boy, belying his forty-five years.

The news bothered him. Since only men were counted in the war census, what was to become of cousin Rizpah's family of women? Visions crowded his mind of Rizpah's begging in the streets of the land bright with promise, with Mahlah beside her on an invalid's pallet. Again his lifelong petition bombarded Elohim's Mercy Seat. *If only she would agree to marry me*. He shook his ruddy hair.

"Trying to shake out the sand flies?" The elder slapped Hanniel's back as he left.

The reserved leader would not normally take such liberties, but Hanniel noticed all the men seemed infected with a festive spirit. The noise of their exuberance, buttressed by the pounding rain, rose and swelled about him. *Who can blame them? All our lives we have awaited this time.*

Hanniel peered out from the tent, squinting eyes the color of brown lentils. Across the Ghor, the rocky desert ascended to fertile hills, a distant, misty obscurity through the downpour. He, too, felt Canaan's beckoning. *Yes, the time is at hand. It will be spring in a few weeks, the time when armies march. And I, along with all Israel, ache to possess the promises. But what of the daughters of Zelophehad? What of Rizpah? What have they to look forward to?*

Hanniel forced his thoughts back to work, and as he focused on the marked stones from the pouch the elder had left with him, his crossed eye stabilized. One by one he called out to his assistant the men each pebble represented, who in turn studiously scratched their names onto broken pottery shards.

"That is all." Hanniel raised his low, raspy tones over the babble of the crowd when they had recorded the last name.

He listened to the fevered talk of war as he waited for his assistant to add today's total to the running figure.

"The tribe of Manasseh numbers 52,700 men of fighting age. We are now sixth in numbers among Israel." The man handed over the shard.

Hanniel gave him a lopsided grin after reading the figure. "It sounds like a festival day in here, doesn't it? Many thanks for your assistance," his voice scraped congenially.

When the man had left, Hanniel stood and stretched, adding momentary height to his average frame. Shaking each foot to renew circulation, he sauntered over to turn in his final figures at the tally booth.

The hard rains flapped the pitched edges of the Tabernacle's Tent of Meeting. All four sides of the Holy Place were drawn up to accommodate the priests and leaders of tribes so that the front tent was nothing more than a huge rain hood. *A very holy rain hood,* Hanniel thought, scanning the Tabernacle, where justice too complicated for the local elders was meted out, and where the people came to inquire of Elohim through Moses. He hesitated when he saw Caleb at the tally booth giving account for his tribe of Judah. Joshua and Caleb's nephew Othniel manned the booth.

"Well, there is no need to worry about Milcah's future. You *are* taking me to her to seek betrothal tonight?" Othniel waited for his uncle Caleb to nod before he went on. "And one of the sisters is already married, and the youngest girl, Tirzah, is betrothed."

"True, most of them will be cared for. But what of the two eldest?" Joshua asked. "There is no chance of any man's marrying the invalid."

"Moses' new use for the census indeed poses unforseen problems," Caleb agreed. "Othniel, I must tell Zelophehad's daughters of this tonight. Can your proposal not wait for a more pleasant occasion?"

"Uncle, I need time to make ready for a wife before we march. There is no time to wait."

Caleb nodded reluctant assent and added absently, "That second-born, Rizpah, is clever. She may have some ideas."

"Clever, yes." Hanniel stepped up and joined the conversation. "And beautiful, is she not?" He addressed only Caleb.

Caleb nodded. "The peace of God be with you, most respected leader of Manasseh."

"And with you, Caleb, mighty leader of Judah. It is a pity the daughters of Zelophehad be denied an inheritance. But, as you say, they will all be cared for by husbands except the two eldest."

"Joshua said that."

Hanniel ignored the comment. "Have you reason to concern yourself with my family's problems?"

"I have. I swore on their father's deathbed I would watch over them until they had no more need of me."

"Is there no other cause for your concern?"

"Do you question me because you are leader of their tribe or their cousin?"

Hanniel stayed his gaze on Caleb and his left eye crossed in concentration. He was satisfied by the strength with which Caleb returned his stare. *There is no hidden guilt in this man,* he acknowledged inwardly. Still, why wouldn't Caleb answer this question? "I question you because *I* have other cause for concern—and you evade my question."

Caleb cleared his throat. "My words may occasion regret, but my silence will avoid it."

"But if speech is the messenger of the heart, what has your heart to regret?"

There was silence. Joshua and Othniel exchanged curious glances behind the booth, as Hanniel and Caleb eyed each other suspiciously.

"Why do you insist on knowing my intentions toward the daughters of Zelophehad?"

"Only toward Rizpah."

"Now you evade *my* question."

"You must know how long I have sought Rizpah for my wife?"

"Zelophehad told me." Caleb gave a stiff nod but his tone was sympathetic.

"Then you know also she will not have me. Her father said it is because she loves you."

"And this angers you?"

Hanniel shook his head. "Marriage to *someone* is the only solution to her problem. You know that." He waited in vain for Caleb's response. "No," he continued. "I would be relieved to hear she was cared for. It is your evasion that angers me."

"In three things is a man's character recognized: in the wine cup, in his purse, and in his anger." Caleb turned to leave and then hesitated, speaking with his back to Hanniel. "If betrothal is used only as the antidote for a problem, then what will ail the marriage may be untreatable."

Though day still lingered in twilight, the heavens were vibrant. Innumerable stars glinted, optimistic of their promised nighttime brilliance, reflecting the mood of the men drifting in to encircle the spitting fire.

Every man in camp anticipated the evenings when, after a satisfying meal, their tribe gathered in an open meeting place. Discussions encompassed any newsworthy topic, the exchange of wisdom in the form of proverbs or riddles, and sometimes heated debate. Tonight, their talk abounded with the coming campaigns against the Canaanites.

Hanniel eased himself against a rock, near enough the fire to ward off the chill of sunset but far enough removed from the inner circle of elders not to be included in the conversation. Relieved to have completed the census that afternoon, he closed his eyes and inhaled the tranquil odor of singed, crackling wood, hoping the conversation would carry him to a place beyond his anxiety for Rizpah. He yearned to play his lyre and ease the grief that rewarded his care for her. Plucking the lyre's strings was the only release he knew, and he sought its refuge often.

"May Elohim grant us victory even while Moses plans our entry into the promised land. Blessed be His name."

"And may God be with our new leader after Moses."

"I expect that Moses will appoint Joshua. There can be no better choice. If our fathers would have harkened to him and Caleb forty years ago, we would now be peacefully settled in the promised land."

Why must I be reminded of Caleb wherever I go? Hanniel opened his eyes and watched the stars shine ever brighter against the curtain of night. *I cannot understand a man who would refuse when a wife such as Rizpah is offered him. I have prayed twenty years to win her and when she is dropped in his lap in the wink of an eye, still he resists.*

Truthfully Hanniel was glad Caleb had bypassed the opportunity. If marriage was her only hope of survival, and there was no other prospective groom, maybe Rizpah would reconsider his proposal. Had he stooped to her desperation as a means to win her?

Once again he dwelt on the first time he had noticed his cousin Rizpah's obvious attraction and the feelings of assurance that seared his heart with the promise of marriage. Could he have been mistaken? Maybe the Lord had *not* promised him Rizpah. Once more he flushed at his presumptuous thoughts, but those hopes persevered, trailing his lovesick heart behind them. As long as Rizpah remained unmarried, he could not marry another.

"But I *need* that land." Hanniel thought he knew the voice that hissed behind him in secrecy. "I have only two sons. Moses will not allot us enough land to sustain the size vineyard I have in mind."

Hanniel had to concentrate to distinguish the raspy whispers that were nearly swallowed by the jubilant wartalk around him.

"Haven't you heard all your life about the size grapes the

spies brought back the first time?" another voice graveled in subdued tones. "Each cluster will produce twice the wine as those in Egypt. Actually you will need only half the plot."

"No, I *need* Zelophehad's portion." At this Hanniel was alert. He recognized the voice belonging to his uncle Salu. "I need land for olive groves, too, and Zelophehad's herds, when added to mine, will require much pasture. The pittance Moses will give me won't sustain half of what I plan."

"But how can you take this land when it does not exist?" Hanniel knew the other voice to be Enosh. "Moses is dividing the land according to the names on the census. With Zelophehad dead, no land will be allotted for him."

"*Unless* I go to Moses and request my brother's name not be cut off in this manner."

"Why? Even if Moses relents, the land still won't be yours."

"Whose will it be?" Salu asked.

"Well, it couldn't go to the daughters. Women cannot own land. It would go to the nearest relative—me." Enosh's voice brightened.

"Right. It would go to you as the eldest, but you would be required to take Rizpah as your wife, and of course, care for Mahlah, too. Do you want another wife and an invalid dependent?"

There was silence. "Puah would make my life miserable."

"And even if you married Rizpah, the land would go to her children by you, not your own sons."

"I do not understand, Salu. If there is nothing to be gained, why would you risk Moses' wrath to request Zelophehad be given land though he is dead?"

"*You* have nothing to gain. I no longer have a wife, and as I said, with only two sons, my portion will be small in Canaan. If you would pass me your sandal before Moses, forfeiting your right to marry Rizpah, I would *graciously* offer to marry the destitute woman and care for her sister."

Hanniel was possessed with a raging desire to fling Salu

into the fire, but he dared not move for fear of discovery. It was impossible to distinguish whether if the heat of his face was from the blaze, or the contempt he felt for Salu. His back tensed in the effort to appear relaxed, and he realized it was numb with cold, or dread.

"You are cunning indeed, Salu, but won't her sons still inherit the land whether she is married to me or you?"

"As your beloved Puah would say, it is such a shame. The poor girl is barren."

"I can see you have thought this out well. Still, what if she won't marry you? She managed to manipulate her weak father out of giving her to Hanniel, and he is leader of all Manasseh. It would have been quite a profitable marriage."

"Zelophehad treated her like a man, as if she had the sense to make decisions; but her father is no longer with us. She will learn that she has no choice. I will teach her."

Hanniel heard the slap of a fist against a palm.

"Besides," Salu continued, "if you support me, there is no alternative for her."

"What about Caleb? He swore to Zelophehad—"

"Bah! Did not our brother practically beg Caleb to marry Rizpah? Ten months have passed with no betrothal announcement. Obviously he doesn't care for her or her fate."

Hanniel flinched. How could Caleb bring such humiliation to Rizpah? Was everyone saying such things about her?

"Why should I risk Moses' wrath along with you? I have no interest in these women. I have not even seen them since our brother's death."

"What would you say to half of all the flock born after the marriage?"

There was a pause. "Would I not need extra pasture to sustain this increased herd?"

Salu chuckled. "We are indeed of the same blood, my brother."

5

Mahlah squinted in the tent's semi-darkness, her fingers forming airy arcs as she jabbed her needle through the heavy silk yoke of Tirzah's bridal dress. Rizpah smiled. She knew Mahlah wouldn't ask her to interrupt her own work. "Do you need to see better, Sister? I can light the lamps, and if I raise the back tent flap you will have the sunset to work by also."

Mahlah looked relieved. "I suppose I do need more light than the rest of you." She indicated the detailed stitches on the yoke. Tirzah looked up from where she and Milcah spun goat hair thread for weaving the mats that would cover her tent floor when she married.

"Oh, Mahlah!" Tirzah crossed the room to inspect her sister's handiwork more closely. "Your hands have wrought work that surpasses a master's. So cunning is your needlework that I could wear nothing beneath it and my nakedness would go unnoticed for the admiration of your embroidery."

"Not by cousin Reuben."

Tirzah blushed. Mahlah shook her finger at Milcah. "Now, now. You must be more discreet. Tirzah is still a virgin maiden."

"And you are not? I see no redness in *your* cheeks," Milcah teased Mahlah.

"Nor in yours, O saucy one."

Rizpah rose and lit the lamps, signaling Milcah to help. She stretched the tent flap high in back of the receiving section while Milcah speared it with two door poles. Sunset's glare swept the room, and so did the late winter breeze. Imagining the warmth of spring, only weeks away, wasn't easy. The four unmarried daughters of Zelophehad's tent tightened their shawls and continued their work resolutely.

Their days were now occupied with Tirzah's imminent wedding, except for the required daily attendance while Moses recited the law. Since Phineas had atoned for idolatry and ended the plague of Baal-Peor by murdering Zimri and the Midianite princess, Cozbi, in their fornication, Moses' preaching increased in fervency and frequency. The people tried to give ear to laws they already knew by heart, but the camp was infused with impatience, talking only of the coming military campaigns. Rizpah sensed that, in all their zeal, they were overlooking something even more essential than a land to call their own. The thrust of Moses' preaching certainly indicated he had similar thoughts.

Rizpah tested the door poles' sturdiness with a shake and, satisfied they would hold, knelt again at the head of a ground loom that ran almost the length of the breezeway. Situating her crossed legs between stone weights that pulled the white vertical warp threads taut over the crossbeam, Rizpah expertly guided red weft threads alternately over and under the warp. She fingered the woven material, envisioning the babies that would one day be bundled in its folds, and the cool nights like this when Reuben and Tirzah would find warmth and privacy beneath it.

Her thoughts habitually regressed to Caleb, and Rizpah commanded herself to stop. *He has made it clear he doesn't want me by his months of silence. I must resign myself to that.* Her aching heart was cheered to watch her youngest sister's beaming face, laboring over articles for her new home; yet,

Rizpah's loss was felt the more because of Tirzah's joy. Rizpah rebuked herself for the thought. *Though I will never know this happiness, I will not begrudge my sister.*

"Look," Tirzah squealed. "Othniel comes—and it is not even the Sabbath." She elbowed Milcah. "It is not only I who may soon give up her maidenhood to marriage."

Tirzah's words brought a stab of guilt to Rizpah. *I've dwelt upon myself so that I haven't even noticed the obvious attraction of Othniel to Milcah. By the look on my lovely sister's face, the attraction is mutual.* Rizpah remembered the night her father died, when Othniel waited so anxiously outside his room to inquire, not after Zelophehad, but Milcah. *How could I have failed to notice before?*

Rizpah followed Milcah's gaze to watch Othniel approach. Ebony hair accentuated his deep tan, and the loose-fitting tunic did little to hide the rippling muscles of his twenty-two-year-old frame. The handsome face, which bore resemblance to his uncle Caleb, gladdened when he spied Milcah through the open front tent flap.

Othniel rounded the neighboring tent, and Caleb strode into view beside him. Rizpah's heart quickened as her previously determined resolves melted. The men stopped at the door to remove their sandals. Othniel's voice hushed as he spoke to Milcah. "Peace on you."

"And on you peace." Milcah blushed as she took his foot to wash it. Othniel greeted no one else, but all forgave his rudeness with knowing smiles.

"The peace bringer comes." Caleb offered the greeting of the sanctuary to them when he was seated upon a striped mat within their circle. The waning sunlight slanted an orange brilliance across his features. He turned to Tirzah. "My joy is made full by the news of your marriage." Tirzah beamed her thanks with lowered head.

Thick waves of Caleb's black hair, salted with silver-gray strands, jutted out from beneath the folded, striped kerchief protecting his head. The soft woolen twist, binding the headscarf in place, seemed to Rizpah a regal crown. She wondered if he would ignore her, just as their eyes met. "Long life to you, Rizpah."

Dared she to believe she heard tenderness in his voice? The gentle lines of secrecy tracing his eyes gave no clues to what lay in his heart. With an angry thrust, Rizpah jammed the shuttle into the warp threads and studiously took up her weaving, unaware that she had failed to return his greeting.

"*Hadtha Beitak*; this is your home, Caleb and Othniel. Please rest and refresh yourselves." Mahlah leaned from her pillows to pour them water.

"By your leave," Caleb addressed Mahlah. "I will state my intent. I have dual purpose in visiting you midweek."

"Yes," Othniel agreed. "We decided to forego the evening fires tonight." He nodded with vigor to emphasize the importance of this absence, though every woman knew how men esteemed their daily meeting time.

Caleb inclined his head toward Othniel and smiled. "I would not have brought my nephew, but I could not prevent it," he teased. "In fact, I was hard pressed to match his pace in coming."

Othniel stared at his feet.

"With your permission," Caleb cleared his throat. "I will begin with the more pleasant of my duties tonight. As Othniel's closest living relative, I have come to seek a betrothal between my nephew and Milcah, daughter of Zelophehad Ben Hepher." He paused.

Milcah could scarce contain her joy but responded with proper gestures of modesty. Even as Milcah's demure head lowered, Rizpah's heart fell. *It's unjust!* she cried inwardly. *How could Caleb speak for my sister's marriage in my presence when he has ignored my confession of love? Is he so cruel?* Rizpah fumed. *No wonder I can read no message of the heart in his eyes. He has no heart.*

Caleb spoke to Mahlah. "As first-born, it is your permission I seek."

Mahlah grabbed Othniel's emptied cup and thrust it high. "Why do our cups hold only water? Where is the wine? Let us drink the cup of the covenant."

Cheers ricocheted off the partitions separating the sleeping quarters that adjoined each side of the receiving section. Rizpah rose and bade her arms to embrace Milcah and her lips to smile, though her heart was dark as the now-fallen night. Shivering in the absence of the sun's warmth, she lowered the front and back tent flaps and refueled the fire.

Tonight she could not run from her smoldering humiliation. Watching Mahlah discharge her betrothal duties from her fleece-covered throne, Rizpah yearned for her comfort, even if it were only the silent solace of the past months. In search of some activity to camouflage her despair and anger, she yanked the huge ground loom aside and removed the baskets of spinning to give the celebrants more room. Fetching the wineskin and additional cups, Rizpah realized her mistake too late. After serving everyone else she stood facing Caleb. Their eyes met as the wineskin's spout touched his upraised cup, but the sparkling liquid remained in the skin.

Caleb cleared his throat. "Rizpah, I..."

She waited but Caleb said no more. Filling his clay mug with trembling hand, she turned to fill her own. Caleb cleared his throat.

The ceremony of solemn promise to unite Othniel and Milcah began, but the scene was a blur to Rizpah. *Caleb acts as if Father's words were never spoken. As if I had not brazenly thrown myself at him that night. As if I don't bear the humiliation of his rejection from every neighbor.* Casting a glance at him, she found he was watching her. She gripped the wine cup to keep from dropping it and concentrated on the porous, earthen mug that felt so cool in her hands. She swished the wine absently, causing the coolness to creep up the rounded sides to her burning fingertips.

"My, my, my. Have we forgotten to observe some feast

this night?" Rizpah jumped as Puah swept into the tent with Enosh and Salu. Puah took in the celebrants and the joyous scene in seconds.

"We are not keeping festival," Mahlah welcomed their seldom-seen relatives, "but you *have* missed the festivities. Join us now. Rizpah, please pour our guests some wine."

Puah accepted the wine along with the men. "What festivities?" she asked.

"Tonight Milcah is the betrothed of Othniel, nephew of Caleb."

"Oh my," Puah gushed to Milcah. "Elohim's favor be forever on your home. May your womb be blessed."

When the congratulations abated Salu bobbed his solemn head. "We are saddened to bring the tidings we bear you on such a night of rejoicing." The group grew silent. Rizpah noticed he kept an eye toward Caleb. "I will be straightforward. As you know, the census was completed today. Are you aware that Moses is using it to allot the promised land before we enter?"

Rizpah glanced at Mahlah, who gave a slow nod. She could tell Mahlah mistrusted the man.

When no one spoke, Salu jerked his arm outright. "Don't you see the significance to you women in this? There are only *men's* names recorded in the census. Your family is not represented."

"Then we will receive no inheritance?" Rizpah's eyes slid to Caleb for confirmation.

Caleb nodded. "This is the other reason for my coming tonight. Would that we could have spoken of it any night other than the betrothal; but I felt you should be told as soon as possible, and Othniel could not be put off another day from his proposal."

Salu smiled through his scraggly beard at the stricken group. "This news need not grieve you. Enosh and I have a solution to the problem." He peered with protruding eyes at each of them before continuing. "We will ask Moses to assign *us* the land that would have gone to your father. Of course, Mahlah and Rizpah may live on the land as if it were their own, and you may all have use of the land. It is the only solution." There was stunned silence while Salu and Enosh smiled and nodded.

"Why are you doing this for us?" Rizpah asked.

Salu opened his mouth, but it was Puah who answered. "My *dear,* you are *family.*"

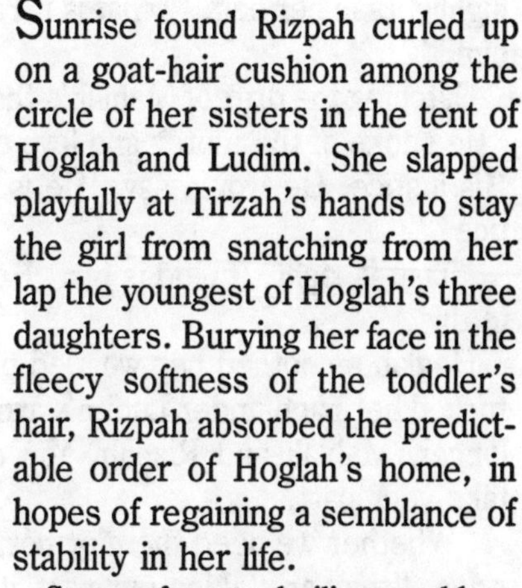

Sunrise found Rizpah curled up on a goat-hair cushion among the circle of her sisters in the tent of Hoglah and Ludim. She slapped playfully at Tirzah's hands to stay the girl from snatching from her lap the youngest of Hoglah's three daughters. Burying her face in the fleecy softness of the toddler's hair, Rizpah absorbed the predictable order of Hoglah's home, in hopes of regaining a semblance of stability in her life.

Steam from a boiling cauldron gathered in clouds near the ceiling, an ominous omen for the day. Milcah ladled gurgling porridge into small bowls, while Mahlah related last night's events to Hoglah and Ludim.

"I wish I could see another remedy to this injustice." Ludim tapped his fingers together.

"*Injustice* is an apt description." Rizpah spoke for the first time.

Mahlah patted her hand. "Be not bitter, Sister."

"Why not?" Ludim's voice was grim. "We are at the mercy of our uncles. Even I cannot intercede, for they are your closest relatives."

Mahlah looked at each hopeless face in the circle, the breakfast firelight bronzing the almond-shell highlights in her hair. "What is it Father so often said of Elohim?"

Catching the drift of Mahlah's thoughts, Rizpah answered. "He spoke of the mercy and love of Elohim, but most of all, His justice. He would say, 'He is most of all a God of justice.' "

"That is right. If God is just, He will surely take our part in this."

Hoglah smoothed her worried brow with a forefinger and tucked her hand under Ludim's arm. "So you must worry no longer, Mahlah and Rizpah. You don't *need* our uncles to take your part."

"Whether we need them or not," Rizpah cupped her porridge, "they are taking our part at the Tent of Meeting this morning."

Milcah handed a steaming bowl to Hoglah. "They *insisted.*"

Ludim stared into his porridge. "I don't trust our uncles."

"Nor I," said Rizpah, voicing her sisters' sentiments also. She stroked the baby's hair. "Even when Father lived they stayed apart from the rest of us. Why would they come to us in our trouble?"

"Because we are *family,*" Milcah's imitation of Puah drew only absent smiles.

"I don't know, but I fear their intent is for ill." Ludim donned his outer coat.

"Where are you going?" Hoglah asked him.

"To the Tabernacle. I want to hear just what our uncles say to Moses."

Rizpah scurried up, tumbling the baby from her lap into Tirzah's waiting arms. "We should all go."

Ludim stared at her.

"I know what you're thinking," Rizpah appealed to him. "Women at the Tent of Meeting? But it is our future that our uncles trifle with. We must see how they deal with us."

Milcah and Tirzah positioned themselves behind Rizpah,

aligning themselves with her protective leadership as they'd done all their lives.

Hoglah still sat at the fire's side. *Independent of us, as usual,* Rizpah thought. Her eyes met Hoglah's, and Ludim's gaze followed.

"Now just wait—" he began.

But no one was listening. They were watching Hoglah rise without breaking eye contact with Rizpah. She turned and picked up her cloak. Rizpah's face broke into a wide grin. For once she and her aloof sister were in unity.

Ludim's stare faltered and he pulled on his sandals. "Do as you wish."

"I will stay with the children." Mahlah waved away her sisters' objections, indicating the chair that Ludim had designed for her. The device made it possible for Mahlah to be conveyed comfortably, but it was awkward. "By the time you carried me there it could be too late. Besides, if Rizpah is there, I am represented. Hurry. May your strength be firm. I fear you'll need it. Remember, Elohim is a God of justice."

The silent group wove through paths cramped between the duplicate black tents of Israel that varied only in size and occupants. The early morning sun warmed Rizpah, reviving hope. Elohim would intervene somehow, just as Mahlah said. He must.

They arrived breathless at the Tabernacle, entering the outer courtyard through a blue, purple, and scarlet linen screen. Rizpah concealed a wary glance as they passed the line of Levites standing guard to prevent unauthorized entrance. Worshipers milled about the open court, waiting for the sacredly arrayed priests to offer up their sacrifices to the Lord.

A priest stood atop the altar in center court, watching with upraised arms the thick billows of black smoke wafting heavenward from the charred carcass. The opaque fumes cast a deathly shadow against the brightly striped walls of linen fencing the courtyard in symbolism of divine protection.

Rizpah and her sisters followed Ludim, skirting the bloody ground beneath the altar where another priest quartered a sheep in preparation for sacrifice, reserving its head and fat. The altar behind the priest already ran with the sprinkled blood of offerings from the continual flow of petitioners, and Rizpah pleaded the favor of Elohim also, though the sacrifice wasn't hers.

Quickly covering the short distance to the Tent of Meeting, they hesitated at the curtained entrance, each summoning a silent courage. Inside, Rizpah blinked, sun dots dancing before her eyes in the sudden darkness of the Holy Place. She should have anticipated the dim interior, considering the roof of goat hair tarpaulin, topped with a layer each of ramskin and badgerskin.

In an effort to adjust her eyes, Rizpah tried to focus on the revered articles of the Holy Place, but the table of the Bread of the Presence was obscured by the crowd, as was the Golden Altar, before which Moses sat each morning to judge the people's cases. The only visible article was the Golden Lampstand, towering above their heads against the south wall, the nightly flames extinguished. Rizpah admired the glinting flowerlike cups, buds, and blossoms of gold that were cast in one piece with the magnificent stand.

She could now make out the faces surrounding her. The Tent of Meeting overflowed with the most important men in the nation, and Rizpah searched for Caleb among them. Scanning the immediate vicinity, she glimpsed her sisters at her side, scarcely lifting their eyes in the presence of such men.

My sisters understand the place of a woman. Here am I, boldly looking into each man's face while they are of modest demeanor. Would that I could be as comely. The regret was fleeting, for Salu's voice came from the direction of Moses. Rizpah squeezed into a position of better observation. Smoke from the Golden Altar stung her eyes as she watched Salu and Enosh kiss the hem of Moses' robe, their stubby frames stiff in the compromising gesture.

Moses presided before the embroidered veil of blue, purple, and scarlet that separated the Holy Place from the Most Holy Place, where the Ark of the Covenant rested. His feet planted a firm span apart, their leader brushed the head of his staff as he listened to Salu.

"So you see, my lord, it is for the welfare of these unprotected women that I seek assignment of the land that would have gone to our brother, and your friend, Zelophehad Ben Hepher."

Rizpah bristled at the injustice of such a man inheriting her Father's land, while the good name of Zelophehad was cut off from Israel. Uncle Enosh removed a sandal and handed it to Salu. Recognizing the symbol of forfeiting the right to marry the nearest relative, Rizpah pressed closer still, her attention full on the proceedings.

Salu held the sandal high. "With this I accept the obligation to marry. Since the eldest daughter is lame and therefore barren, I will take Rizpah to wife and pledge to care for the eldest daughter all the days of her life."

Rizpah whirled to see Ludim's reaction, but with all her maneuvering she had lost sight of him. She took a calming breath, clenching tight fists, but panic overtook her. *This must be stopped,* she shouted inwardly. Done in the presence of witnesses, this act was compulsory if not challenged. No one in the tabernacle moved to her defense, not even Elohim. *Has the God of justice forsaken me?*

Salu's disgusting voice boomed. "You have all witnessed the passing of the sandal. So let it be."

"No! It cannot be!" Realizing she had shouted the words aloud, Rizpah knew she must now see her own case through. The men around her gawked incredulously as she shoved through them to fall on her face before Moses.

"I beg you, my lord. Allow me to speak." Her breath disturbed the dusty carpet, and she gulped sand granules that gritted between her teeth as she pleaded.

Murmurs arose from the group of men in the Tent of Meeting. Never before had a woman sought to represent herself in the council, and Rizpah feared the reprisal for defying tradition. Casting caution aside, she blurted, "I don't wish to be his wife," before Moses had granted permission for her to speak.

Hanniel heard the surrounding men gasp as indignant whispers circulated.

"*Mashallah!* What has God done?"

"Next she will want to choose wives for our sons."

Hanniel wiped beads of sweat from his upper lip. He had planned to foil Salu's plot himself, but when the moment came, he was as stone. Not that he feared a man like his uncle, but he was not fleet of speech. Words failed him when he needed them most, and now he had failed Rizpah.

"Please, my lord. May I speak?" Rizpah begged again from her prostrate position.

Moses tugged at his long, white beard, considering the woman before him. "Rise and speak."

Rizpah stood, brushing the sand from her clothes, keeping her eyes cast respectfully downward.

"How dare you defy me?" Salu growled.

"Silence," Moses commanded Salu, and then to Rizpah, "Speak."

A strand of burnt umber hair fell over her high forehead, obstructing her view. She puffed at it, but the humidity of the crowded meeting tent held it firmly in place. A nervous swipe removed the offending hair but left grains of sand plastered to her forehead. Hanniel willed her strength.

"Our father died in the wilderness, but he did not perish in Korah's revolt, thus losing his inheritance. He revered Ha-Elohim and His servant, Moses, but he had no sons."

Pride kindled in Hanniel's chest as the woman he loved squared her shoulders and lifted her eyes to look directly into Moses'. She spread her arms and her voice rang clear.

"I ask, why should the name of Zelophehad be wiped from Israel as footprint in a sandstorm, because he bore only daughters? Why should the family of Salu be burdened with the care of two women? My father's inheritance should be given directly to his daughters. It is rightfully ours."

Rizpah clapped a hand over her mouth, her dark eyes bulging amber saucers in an ashen face as she realized how far she had gone in her own defense. Hanniel feared for her safety as the tent erupted with objections.

"Women cannot own land."

"The woman should be stoned for her defiance."

"She questions Elohim as Korah did."

Moses stared at the woman holding her face in her hands. His uplifted right arm silenced the men. He stroked his beard with his right hand and rubbed the knob of his staff with his left, while the room grew quiet. Rizpah's shivers vibrated the hem of her ankle-length tunic.

"I will bring your case before Yahweh."

Moses used the name for Elohim that no one else dared use, underscoring his authority. The men of the Tabernacle sucked in their breath of one accord and held it in shocked silence.

Rizpah wavered. Three strides brought Hanniel to her aid, to meet Caleb at her side. He glared at the man who he felt caused Rizpah's plight. Caleb seemed to sense the blame in Hanniel's eyes and retreated into the crowd, before the dazed Rizpah was aware of his presence.

Manasseh's leader lifted the headscarf that had fallen to Rizpah's shoulders and covered her head with it. His action guaranteed protection. No one would interfere with her exit when she was escorted by Hanniel. He touched her elbow. "Let me take you to your tent."

Out in the Tabernacle's crowded courtyard, the sun's brilliance and the acrid sacrificial smoke jolted Rizpah from her trance-like state. She blinked at Hanniel. "May you be blessed of Elohim for delivering me from *them*." They glanced back at the mob congregated just outside the Tabernacle's curtain, murmuring and glaring at her. Hanniel took her elbow and steered her outside the courtyard. Freeing herself from his grip, she repeated her blessing and added, "But I need to be alone."

"You need to be comforted," Hanniel said, looking startled at his own words. "You are still shaking."

"Perhaps you are right." Rizpah threw him a nervous smile and then stared over the points of the black sea of tents toward the pink Moab mountains. "I never expected Moses to speak as he did. I thought I would be rebuked—if not now, then later. Moses has only postponed my punishment. I have brought shame to my family. Don't take me home. I don't think I can face them."

The crowd of hostile men now grumbled and peered at them through the screen of the fenced courtyard. Hanniel touched her arm. "Let us go further outside camp." As he led her westward, Rizpah withdrew. "What is it?" he asked.

She pointed toward the distant Ghor. "I don't want to face the promise of the Jordan. There may be no promise for me. Let us go to the east of camp, facing the mountains from whence we have come. Then I may look back on a time when there was hope."

Again the shawl had fallen to her shoulders. Her hair was clasped into the traditional knot at the nape of her neck, but loosened wisps trailed in the wind. The sun now arced above them with ever increasing heat. Though only late morning, the burnt orange rocks and sand approached white-hot.

Rizpah halted. Her firm chin lifted as she studied the soaring heights of the fertile Moab mountains. After awaiting in vain for Hanniel's promised comfort, she finally broke the silence, flinging her arms wide. "My tongue has slit my throat once more, and this time not only mine, but my sisters' as well. When will I learn my place?"

"You—you did what you thought right."

"*Right?* You saw those men. They care not if I am right.

They saw only my insubordination. Not even Elohim came to my defense. I must have sinned terribly for my God to desert me." A picture of woe, she spread her arms to the mountains and asked of them, "Was it so wrong for a woman to take up her own case before Moses? To desire security in the land of promise? Am I not also a child of Israel?"

Hanniel reached out and, with a slightly trembling touch, brushed away the sand still clinging to Rizpah's forehead. She retreated a step from his advance. "Forgive me," he blurted. "I don't know why I—"

Rizpah retreated another step. *Is this how he comforts me?* she thought. *By adding to my despair?*

"No, that's not true, Rizpah. I do—do know why."

Rizpah turned from his explanation. He took a step closer, his voice husky and halting. "I've always gone to your father with this request before. But—"

"Don't." Rizpah clapped her hands over her ears.

Hanniel stopped. The hoarseness of his voice thickened. "You still wait for Caleb, don't you?"

Rizpah snorted. "After I laid my heart before him he thinks me as brazen as the Moabite and Midianite women."

"But still you wait?" he pressed.

Rizpah turned and studied his face. He looked like a lost little boy, with his one eye slightly crossed and tassels of fawn-colored hair blowing around his wind-chapped cheeks and broad shoulders. He was of the same height as she, so there was no need to look up to face him as she did Caleb, but she felt compelled to look away. He ran calloused fingers through his russet hair. "That man is a fool," he muttered.

Rizpah clenched her fists, a burst of anger prompting her. "He is no fool. He may be the wisest of the men of Israel—a quality I admire and covet." Her eyes misted as she watched drifting pink clouds kiss the mountaintops. Her voice was an absent whisper and she spoke as if to herself, from somewhere within.

"Let other women have the thrill of beauty for a moment

before it fades, or the praise of the industry of their hands before they become feeble and cramped, or be exalted by the number of heirs they provide their husbands before their wombs close. Let them possess these things, but give me wisdom.

"Wisdom doesn't fade with age and cease to attract, it does not quell productivity when age infirms the body, or cease when the monthly flow issues no more. Even death cannot kill wisdom, for it lives in the lives touched by it, in the lives of those who also crave after wisdom's treasure.

"And Caleb possesses this. He has never tried to prove his wisdom; perhaps that is why it is so evident. He courted wisdom, and she hearkened to his call and found refuge in his anxious arms. I only pray that one day wisdom will welcome my embrace. And that Caleb may also." Her last words were barely audible.

"You cherish this hope still? Even after...?"

Rizpah started at the sound of Hanniel's gruff voice. Embarrassed at her own rambling, her tone became curt. "I've tried to quench my hope, but I cannot."

Hanniel looked long into her eyes. "The man is a fool," he repeated with vehemence.

"He is certainly wiser than you, who discard your youth waiting for one to marry you who never will."

Injury clouded Hanniel's eyes. Rizpah broke their gaze. She paced off a short step and back to face him, wringing her hands. "I am sorry, Hanniel. At times I wish I could rip out my lashing tongue. I didn't want to hurt you.

"You see, I look into your eyes and I recognize your suffering. We are family in more than blood, my cousin. We are of the tribe of the persistent. Our expectations wither slow. An acacia tree deprived of its water still lives on, as does our hope deprived of reason. I spoke sharply that I might uproot your acacia of hope. The pain is severe, but it is over more quickly this way. I cannot bear that I cause your tree an endless death by drought."

"What of *your* drought? Perhaps I cannot water you with the rain your acacia desires, but can I not be to you as an underground spring?"

Rizpah shook her head. "I also know parching, but that is why I seek to prevent yours."

Hanniel stepped closer, his hoarse voice falling to a whisper. "There is still your endangered inheritance. What if Moses denies your request? You will need a man to care for you and Mahlah. That has been my life's desire." He touched her shoulder, his words stuttering. "If we married now, I could wait for your love to—"

"No." She pulled from his touch.

"Even if you never grow to love—"

"Stop it."

After a silence, Hanniel conceded to the truth. "You can never love me because of Caleb." His words were not a question.

Rizpah looked him full in the face, her eyes blurred with weariness. "Perhaps it is time we both uproot our acacias." Draping her shawl over her hair, she turned, leaving Hanniel as drained of hope as she was.

7

A full, rising moon bathed the outdoor wedding feast of Reuben and Tirzah in a brilliant white glare. Even with the moon's illumination, torches had been tied aloft acacia branches and planted in a flaming circle, within which celebrants danced, and around which feasters reclined. A small crescent of torches outlined the musicians in a burning stage within the larger circle, and separated the men and women dancers. Their thunderous celebration nearly drowned out the whine and beat of the band.

The desert wanderers' drab, everyday garb tonight was exchanged for plumage that would have shamed a peacock, accompanied by shouts and laughter nearly as colorful. So great was the people's riotious exuberance that the earth would surely rend with the sound of them.

Folding her arms, Rizpah oversaw the feast with great relief, stepping into the role at Mahlah's request. When she had learned that many of her father's friends, men of high station in Israel, had declined their invitation to the wedding because of her defiance at the Tabernacle two weeks ago, she feared the feast would be another humiliation she had caused her family to suffer. However, when Moses himself was one of the first guests to arrive, word spread as a sirocco wind, and the stately elders now paraded before her. The joyous event was not spoiled for Tirzah after all. Her sister would cherish this night forever in her heart. *For once I have done right.*

Checking again on the food preparation before attending to Mahlah's needs, she headed for the spits and sand ovens outside the circle of flames. Amorite slaves scurried about, basting and slicing the quails, kids, and calves roasted to perfection. The foreigners, captives from the Transjordan wars, served Israel by carrying water and attending to feasts. They had brought with them varieties of vegetables, herbs, and condiments that now tantalized Rizpah's nose, reminding her of her hunger. *Yet another touch that makes Tirzah's wedding the grandest my generation has seen.*

Shutting out the noise of the crowd, Rizpah inhaled the exotic aromas. A warm, yeasty scent overpowered the succulent smell of roasting meats, and she opened her eyes to see a servant stumble past under the burden of a huge tray of assorted breads. Demonstrating that forty years of limited ingredients could not quench their culinary abilities, the women of Israel had quickly renewed their skills in the art of bread making and provided the guests with a sample of their artistry this night. Rizpah trailed the tempting array of crisp discs covered with sesame and coriander seeds, paste-bun triangles stuffed with pounded almonds, twisted rope coils of pasta steeped in a sauce of honey and nuts, and thin wafers coated with grape syrup and powdered with pungent seeds and leaf dust. Following the servant brought her to the women's portion of the circle. She squatted beside Mahlah. "How do you fare, Sister? Are you in any need?"

Mahlah laughed. "No, no, I've never been so full—and I don't speak only of my belly." She held her hand over her heart. "Just look at our littlest sister. Is she not the most beautiful bride in Israel?" She swept an arm toward the dancing women.

Tirzah minced and twirled amid giggling maidens, her petite form glazed with the shimmering silk of her embroidered wedding garment. The bride's laughter tinkled through the clear night air, even when she vanished among the rainbow blur of the dancers' swirling skirts. When she came again into view she could be seen peering across the circle of torches to meet her new husband's searching gaze.

"The most beautiful bride in Israel?" Rizpah poked Mahlah's ribs. "In the history of our people!"

Mahlah laughed agreement and pulled on her sister's sleeve, tumbling her from her squatting position. At Rizpah's squeal, Mahlah pressed her down firmly. "You have worked enough. Sit. Eat." She thrust a steaming bowl of red lentils at Rizpah.

Only a whiff of the onion-and-garlic-seasoned beans convinced her of the wisdom of Mahlah's suggestion. She was ravenous. No sooner was she properly seated than servants hustled to offer her lamb, breads, nuts and grapes and olives, fresh milk, minted water, and wine. Rizpah refused nothing, eating in pure enjoyment until she was stuffed.

Mahlah tossed a pistachio into her mouth. "You see? I was right, was I not? You should have eaten long ago."

Satisfied, Rizpah took one last, long draught from the skin of wine incessantly passed among the guests, and sighed. Immediately, from habit, her eyes scanned the crowd for sight of Caleb. She need not look long. The eighty-year-old man hopped and laughed among the dancing youths of Israel as if he were hardier than they.

I live only to see Caleb, she sighed in resignation to her fate. *No matter how I try not to, and no matter what the future brings, I can love no other.* The thought was more bitter than sweet, for though love soothes as honey, unrequited love sears the soul as a flame to the bee hive. Rizpah's breast was filled with both.

The strings of lyres, harps, and Phoenician zithers plunked melodious vibrations, while the staccato beat of hand drums and clanging metal cymbals pounded an enticing rhythm through the brisk, spring night air. Above all, the shrill timbre of the double-reed pipes droned in strident tones that blended a spiritual quality into the softer toned flutes. A burst of laughter erupted from the men's quarters. Three rowdy youths, obviously uninhibited by the wine, pulled Hanniel from his seat, shouting encouragement.

"What do they do?"

"They want him to play the lyre for us." Mahlah clapped. "Haven't you ever heard him? He plays well."

Rizpah saw Hanniel smile and lift his hands as if to ward off the invitation. "But I cannot. I don't have my lyre."

As if by magic, the beautiful instrument appeared. He reached for his possession as if the giver had violated him by touching it. Hanniel's cinnamon eyes shone as he stroked the polished side arms, which curved up from the square sounding board to join with a crossbar at the top. Plucking the ten strings, fastened in a cluster at the bottom of the sounding board, and strung in a widening fan to the crossbar, he argued, less convincingly. "I have nothing prepared."

Rizpah could tell he loved the instrument and added her applause to the crowd's. As she clapped, Hanniel's eyes met hers. His russet hair was set aflame by the surrounding torchlight, luring a ruddy blush into his cheeks and forehead. "Very well." He gave Rizpah a lopsided grin over the torches and took a seat among the musicians. "*Al mahalat,*" he cued them as he accepted the tiny plectrum to stroke the strings.

The band took up an immediate, sorrowful refrain in response to his cue. Hanniel didn't break in with a plunge and a pluck, but eased in skillfully, with the grace of a mountain stream entering a valley pool. Gradually, continually, his strumming intensified until he threw down the plectrum, sweeping the ten strings with both hands.

Words poured from his throat in familiar hoarseness, but in song the raspy tones wrung indescribable emotions from the depths of Rizpah. The gruff contrast bespoke a tender mourning of something regrettable, something lost—nay, something irretrievable.

Rizpah examined the features of this man who she knew still loved her, despite her discouragement. Two weeks ago she could not have realized such depth from his bumbling attempt to comfort her, but she understood now that what he lacked in speech, he made up for in music. Rizpah viewed Hanniel through new eyes.

Torchlight flickered over his wide nostrils, quivering in song. His thick, sensitive lips caressed the haunting melody, and his face was a circle of mystery and enticement above the embrace of his lyre. Hanniel was attractive enough that maidens of Manasseh continually sought to marry him; yet, Rizpah had always found his face unexciting and bland, like unseasoned lentils. But tonight...

"Mistress?" a servant whispered to Rizpah.

"Yes?"

"I have a message for you to meet Caleb of Judah in the Tent of Meeting."

Rizpah stared at Mahlah, who shook her head. "I know nothing of it."

Ducking out of the moonlit edges of the wedding party, her eyes met Moses'. She thought he winked at her. *Surely it is only the torchlight's reflection.*

The Tabernacle was deserted. Not even the illumination of the full moon penetrated the insulated ceilings of the Tent of Meeting. The only light was from the Golden Lampstand, throwing divergent shadows across the room at will, slicing the silence with its flames. Rizpah felt chilled.

"Caleb?"

"I am here."

Rizpah whirled at the sound of his voice behind her. He stepped from the shadows of the tent door, but said nothing.

"Should we be here?" Rizpah indicated the Holy Place.

"I have Moses' permission."

At the mention of their leader, she was alert. "Has this to do with Moses?"

"Yes, I have spoken with him. He took your appeal before Elohim and has heard from the Most High."

In the following silence, Rizpah searched his eyes for the answer she had awaited with dread these past two weeks, but she could find no clues there. He only watched her. She shifted her weight, and still he stared. She probed again with her eyes but he was silent. She could wait no longer. Doubling her fist, she pummeled his arm, waiving formalities with him. "Will you tell me or not?"

Caleb laughed, startling her. "I told Moses I wished to be the one to tell you the news, but I didn't know I was inviting battle. I should have guessed the first night under the stars, when you growled at me because you found this plain unfavorable, that I was in the presence of a tigress. Is no one safe from you?"

"You are teasing me," Rizpah stated, amazed at Caleb's camaraderie.

At Rizpah's beseeching look, he relented. "All right, I will tell you. The Lord said you are right."

"I am right?"

"You are right." Caleb laughed again.

"The land is ours?"

"The land is yours."

Rizpah wavered. Caleb's arm steadied her. *What is he saying? I was right? The elders of Israel rebuked me with their shunning, and Elohim has declared I was right? Uncle Salu publicly denounced me, and the Lord Elohim declares I was right?* She turned a stunned face to Caleb. "Is this a dream?"

"No, Rizpah. And not only that, Elohim has ordered a new law made that if any man dies and leaves no son, his inheritance must go to his daughters."

"But women cannot own land."

"This day they can." Caleb threw an arm high. "Rizpah,

do you realize what you have wrought? This day, a new law is made in Israel. You stood for justice, and now daughters can own land."

"I stood for justice?" Rizpah echoed, reminded of her father's prophetic words. *You will stand for justice, and justice will circumcise you.* Now she understood. These two weeks she had thought surely she would be cut off. But now...

"You stood for justice," Caleb affirmed, touching her chin to guide her gaze back to him. His voice was low. "I knew I admired you since that night last summer beneath the stars. I gave you opportunity to deny your father's words gracefully, about your feelings for me." Rizpah winced at the painful memory, but Caleb kept a firm hold of her chin. "Though you risked humiliation, you were truthful. That took great courage, the kind of courage that caused me no surprise when you stood against your uncle."

Caleb's eyes traced her features, softened by the dim lamplight in the Tabernacle. He lowered her shawl from her head and smoothed her hair. Rizpah's heart pounded and her breath came in short gasps. "Do you know how beautiful you are?" He continued before she could blush. "My heart has long resisted you, but you battle agressively even in love. It is true: no one is safe from you, not even I."

The lampstand's light was blocked from view by his bent head. Rizpah felt warmth across her cheek, and then Caleb's lips touched hers, soft and lingering. She gulped, her disbelieving eyes huge nuggets of gold in the lamplight. "Then you do—"

"Love you?" Caleb cleared his throat. "I think so. I must. If you could know what I felt when I watched you stand against your uncle and the traditions of the council. I knew you were right, even then. Even as I knew forty years ago I was right to stand with Joshua against the other spies. If you could only know what I feel for you...."

"I do know. I do." Rizpah was breathless. "I feel the same for you. I always have."

The veil was lifted from Caleb's eyes, and there she found fear. "And will you always feel so? I am so much older than—"

Rizpah covered Caleb's lips with her slim fingertips. "I always will."

She put the promise of her heart into those words; still, the fear remained and refused to retreat, even when Caleb asked, "Well, then, will you be my child bride?"

Rizpah laughed. "Can one be a child at thirty-nine?"

"If anyone can, it is you." Caleb's head bent once more and sent bolts of lightning through her with the brush of his lips against hers.

8

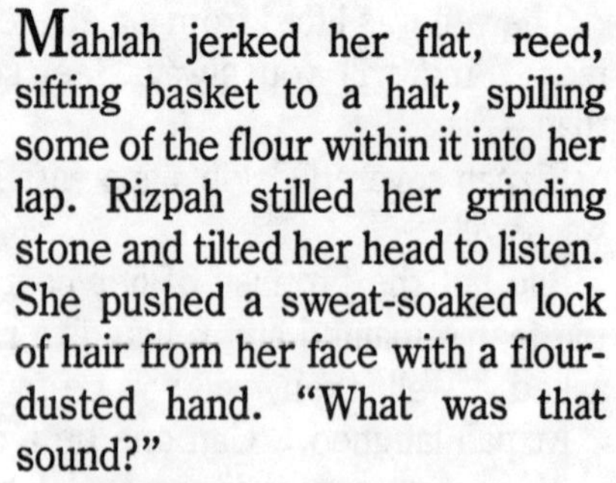

Mahlah jerked her flat, reed, sifting basket to a halt, spilling some of the flour within it into her lap. Rizpah stilled her grinding stone and tilted her head to listen. She pushed a sweat-soaked lock of hair from her face with a flour-dusted hand. "What was that sound?"

"I think it is..."

The blare of a distant shofar, the ram's horn used to announce all the nation's events, was unmistakable this time, and it sounded the victory call. Mahlah and Rizpah let loose a wild cheer and grabbed for eath other. "We have won!" Mahlah reached up to squeeze her sister. "Our army returns victorious from our last battle east of the Jordan."

Hugging herself, Rizpah pranced and swirled around her reclining sister until the grinding stone toppled, sheeting the floor mat with flour.

"Oh, no. Our whole morning's work is ruined."

"I care not." Rizpah laughed and did a jig upon the scattered flour. "Let the captive Moabite and Midianite women grind our grain. They made slaves of the men of Israel in their orgy rituals at Peor. Let them now be made *our* slaves."

Mahlah clapped her hands. "Here." She threw a bag full of flour across the woven carpet. "Let the foreign women supply us with new grain also."

Rizpah squealed at the tide of flour and trampled it with fervor. The slap of hundreds of sandals rushing past the tent was added to the patter of her dance and spurred her to action. "I must fetch Milcah from grazing the flocks. I need her to help carry your chair."

"No. Go to meet the army without me. I am a heavy burden in such a distance and amid the crowds. Besides, the leaders of Manasseh would be well pleased at my absence."

"Moses has said that the leaders of each family must go to help divide the spoils. You are the first-born and head of our clan." Rizpah headed for the door.

"But my chair is so troublesome...."

Rizpah shooed her sister's objection with the wave of a hand and ducked out the tent door. The jubilant flood of neighbors swept her into their stream. She heard her name shouted above the acclaims of the people, but the flow prevented her from turning. "Rizpah, betrothed of Caleb," the voice shouted again. With great effort, using her arms as rudders to shift direction in the river of Israelites, she grasped hold of a tent pole.

Caleb caught up to her and beamed. "I think I like the sound of that."

"And I." She blushed.

"Are you on your way to meet the army outside camp?"

"No, I—"

"Rizpah," Caleb interrupted. "You must not let the hostility of the elders deter you. Let them wag their tongues like old widows. Mahlah is head of your family, and you must take her whenever Moses calls for Israel's leaders."

Rizpah's smile bordered on a smirk. "I was going to say, sir, that I am headed for the pastures to fetch Milcah and bid her help me carry Mahlah to meet the army."

Caleb cleared his throat. "Do not trouble Milcah. I will help you carry your sister."

"I am grateful for your aid." Rizpah winked. "*And* your inspiring speech."

Caleb cleared his throat.

Outside camp, Rizpah and Caleb lowered Mahlah's chair to the sand. The sea of men representing the heads of all Israel's clans was so dense they could come no closer to where Moses and the High Priest Eleazer awaited the approaching army. Rizpah checked on Mahlah's comfort and then began a series of short hops in an attempt to see over the waves of turbans and headscarves. "The shofar tells me the army is near. Oh, how I wish I could see." She tugged on Caleb's sleeve as she jumped.

"Aha!" Caleb retrieved his sleeve from her grip. "It is not my cloak that is to be divided as booty."

Rizpah laughed, throwing back her head. The drab shawl dropped from her hair, unveiling a halo of illuminating bronze highlights. She smoothed it back with both hands and held it tight at the nape, hugging her neck in anticipation.

Caleb looked around and then motioned to her left. "Here, stand on this boulder."

Rizpah skipped onto it, checking her balance when the boulder tipped. She squinted her eyes, searching the eastern horizon for the returning victors. "I see them, Caleb. Mahlah, they come from there." She pointed eastward.

Twelve thousand men, a thousand from each tribe of Israel, returned dancing in the sweltering midday sun. "They come shouting and singing, each tribe bearing its own standard." Rizpah shaded her eyes and scanned the troops. "There is Manasseh's banner." She pointed out the black flag with an embroidered figure of a wild ox, though she knew her companions could not see it.

She wiped the perspiration from her forehead. The sun beat down with such intensity she could scarce breathe. Glancing at the top of Caleb's head beside her, she wondered if the *heat* was that which stole her breath.

She turned her attention back to the troops and continued

her narration. "Behind the army march a multitude of Moabite and Midianite women. I hear them bemoaning their captivity. Can you hear?" Rizpah's heart momentarily ached for them, until she reminded herself that these women were who had caused this war of vengeance. These women had infiltrated their camp and seduced the men of Israel with their clinging tunics and incense and perfume, tempting the men to join their orgy rituals by flirting and sashaying through camp, bringing Israel's men under their spell. Now, their wails fell on unhearing ears, unsympathetic hearts. Justice had served them.

The shofar blasted repeatedly, the deafening blare upon them now. Rizpah trembled. She clasped her hands as the waves of heat and victory crashing against her. "They have returned." She grabbed Caleb's hair in her excitement. "Moses now receives them. The prisoners fall on their faces. Our warriors are triumphant!" She pounded her fist on Caleb's head and jumped up and down. The boulder rocked her to the ground. Caleb reached for her but missed. Laughing, he sank to the ground beside her, rubbing his abused head.

"I fear you have emptied my head with your assault." His eyes grew tender. "But it is no matter. You have filled my heart."

Rizpah touched Caleb's cheek, and gratitude replaced the mirth in her eyes. "Until I had you, my life was not. I walked in my body's steps, performed my duties, slept in my bed, but I abided in a living death, existing only for the day you would return my love. But life, real life was not found here," she crossed her heart with her hand. "Now, your love has made me live."

Caleb held her gaze. He seemed to invite her into the soul his eyes protected, but then he was closed to her. He cleared his throat. "It is true, my love. Not even I am safe from you."

7

The humidity of deepening spring was more evident amid the throng of Manasseh's leaders crowded into Hanniel's small tent. Rizpah wiped the sweat from her upper lip with the sleeve of her coarse wool tunic. She sat silently on the floor beside Mahlah, the two women making themselves as unobtrusive as the sand beneath the carpets.

Casting timid glances about her and inclining her ear to the hum of the men's conversation, Rizpah could fathom no reason for this meeting other than the resultant zeal of yesterday's victory over the Moabites and Midianites. Had Hanniel not invited them, she and Mahlah would not have known the tribal leaders called this council. After a quick survey of the garrulous elders of Manasseh, she suspected the oversight was purposeful. The men still resented Mahlah's representing the clan of Zelophehad, with Rizpah as her mouthpiece.

Rizpah watched Mahlah out of the corner of her eye. She looked so dignified and composed, propped in her fleece-lined chair, but Rizpah knew the fear that prevented her sister's speaking her mind before these men. Mindful of the simple wisdom of that silent mouth, Rizpah pitied the leaders who denied Mahlah's council, for the loss was theirs.

Her gaze caught Hanniel's. She was puzzled by his expression. The russet hair around his forehead darkened with perspiration, and he adjusted the twisted rope of his headband to absorb the moisture. Squirming upon the small rug beneath him, he turned his attention toward the elder, Jair, with what seemed to Rizpah like reluctance.

"Honored leaders of Manasseh." Jair coughed as he stood. "Revered elders of the tribe that ranks sixth in strength of numbers among Israel—my brethren." Long, black locks of hair hid his ruddy cheeks as he bowed in greeting. "As you all know, the tribes of Gad and Reuben are to request that the land of Moab, Ammon, and Gilead be allocated as their inheritance." There was a knowledgeable buzz in response.

"But I say to you, my brethren," Jair pointed a finger out the door toward the offending tribes, "that they have no right to claim alone all land east of the Jordan, toward the sunrise. Who are the fearless warriors who took the lead when Israel attacked these kingdoms in might and victory?" This time he gestured toward the men within the tent.

"Manasseh!" they cheered.

Rizpah turned to Mahlah and whispered, "Did you know of this?" Mahlah shook her head and put a finger to her lips to signal Rizpah to silence. As Rizpah turned back to listen, she was surprised at the dark expression on Hanniel's face.

"Then I ask you," Jair crossed his muscular arms, "are not we entitled to a portion of this lush land also?"

"We are." A clan leader called Nobah jumped to his feet. "Will we be silent while the men of Gad and Reubenites prosper on the land we helped to conquer?"

"But, Nobah, Jair!" Hanniel spoke for the first time. "If we follow your line of reasoning, we would claim a portion of all the land we will help conquer when we march on Canaan."

"That is true," interjected the leader named Hul. "What

right have we to claim land east of the Jordan? Only Canaan has been promised us by Elohim." There were halting mutters of agreement.

"The Lord God of Israel sent us to battle for these eastern lands and gave us victory. Would *He,*" Jair pointed at the roof, "deny us our possession?"

Hul glared at him across the tent. "Do you dare to disdain our promised inheritance? Would you risk sparking the Lord's wrath with your rejection?"

Jair opened his mouth to counter, his eyes flashing, but Nobah laid a restraining hand on his arm and answered Hul himself. "Not *reject* our promised land, only *request* already conquered land north in the lush Bashan of Gilead." He turned from Hul and addressed the assemblage. "The men of Gad and Reuben are profitable shepherds; they know what is fertile land. That is why they desire to settle east of the Jordan. Manasseh is a tribe of warriors, but will not our flocks also increase in Gilead? Will not our vineyards prosper in Bashan, too?"

"No." Rizpah thumped her chest with her fist. "How can you talk of forfeiting our allotment in Canaan? We risked everything to gain that inheritance. You will not take it from us."

The eye of every man present turned upon Rizpah and Mahlah, scorching them with the heat of hostility. In the silence Rizpah could hear the pawing of tethered camels outside. She reached for Mahlah in an instinctive embrace.

"No one will take anything from anyone," Hanniel assured, his gruff voice taut with authority, now free from stuttering. "I will tell you, though: I do not approve this talk of denying our promised inheritance." The support of Hul that was only halting before, strengthened behind Hanniel. Once more, as on the night of Tirzah's wedding, Rizpah was impressed with another facet of her cousin's character. She knew now why Hanniel seemed reluctant to start the meeting.

Hul spoke again to Jair and Nobah, the veins of his temples

straining. "Do you realize the danger of this talk? If you indeed approach Moses with this request, you will call down not only *his* anger on us all, but that of Elohim as well."

"If you go before Moses," an angry voice cried out, "you will go alone. We will not support this folly."

"Nor will we. There have been enough delays. Let us concentrate on the occupation of Canaan."

"You have our support, Jair," shouted three men next to Rizpah.

"And ours. We have done nothing to be fearful before God."

The tent erupted into volcanic argument, divided, it seemed to Rizpah, in half. Amid the heated battle she turned to Mahlah for comfort. "This," she indicated the confusion with one hand and leaned on Mahlah's chair. "Just when I thought our future was stable. For what did we fight?"

"For a possession." Mahlah leaned toward Rizpah to be heard over the insults and curses flying between the men. "Does it matter where that possession is?"

Rizpah caught her breath. "Not you, too?" She stared at the serene invalid beside her.

Mahlah laid her hand on Rizpah's and spoke gently. "I am weary, Rizpah. The thought of war, stretching for years before me, the prospect of traversing another country in this body..." She indicated her lifeless legs and sighed. "Not knowing when we can make permanent camp...I cannot face such a life any longer. I need rest. I do not believe Elohim will be angry with me for requesting this rest in Gilead."

"We will be separated by such a great distance when I marry Caleb and live in Canaan among the inheritance of Judah."

"We would have been separated anyway."

Not if your stubborn pride relented and you would agree to live with me and Caleb, Rizpah thought. Studying Mahlah's noble profile, she knew there was not much chance of that.

"But all we fought for...all we have gained..."

"We will still possess. Whether in Canaan or in Gilead, our father's name will live among Israel. That is what we fought for; that is what we gained." Mahlah patted her hand. "I know what you are thinking, and you can stop. You remember our widowed cousin Nathan?"

"You mean the sad one?"

"Yes. He *is* sad, and because of this I think he will ask me to marry him. He is so lonely, and I think I can be good company for him. So you needn't worry. I will be cared for when you are gone."

Rizpah was not surprised at the announcement. The kind man had spent many hours at their tent of late. The two sisters looked deeply into each other's eyes, as if they were this moment saying good-bye. "Is this then the decision you wish voiced for our clan?"

Mahlah nodded. Rizpah straightened her shoulders and cast her voice into the din. "Enobled leaders of Manasseh, hear me! I know you would not give heed to a woman, but please allow me to speak for the clan of Zelophehad, and for Mahlah, our leader." Every eye turned upon her again. Waves of frothy silence broke over Rizpah in swell after overwhelming swell. She hurried on to fill the gap. "Though we cast our lot with those who wish to settle in Gilead, please, let us cease this striving." Rizpah noted the shocked expression on Hanniel's face. *He must have counted on our support,* she realized, surprised at the regret she felt in disappointing him.

"And what would you have us to do?" trilled a man imitating a female voice. He continued in normal toncs. "I think the daughter of Zelophehad heeds the saying, 'When there is no man, be thou the man.' Think you, Rizpah, that you are the only man present?" Voices rose in heated indignation.

"That was not my intent, my lords. I only meant that we must not divide ourselves thus." The men were not listening. Their purposeful twisting of her intentions angered her, and she raised her voice above their badgering. "Does not a saying also go, 'He who is first silent in a quarrel springs from a good family'?"

Astonished silence filtered the tent. Rizpah took a deep breath, her anger abating. "I meant no offense to any of you, but I do ask: what cause do we have to fight among ourselves like this?"

"And *I* ask again, what would you have us do?" Rizpah's heckler rejoined, but this time the crowd was not quick to join in. Instead, they watched her.

"We can find something to do." Rizpah faltered, realizing they expected her to tell them what, to prove her worth. "There is always *something* we can do."

Hostile murmurs rippled through the crowd, and the men seemed in one accord to shift to the other foot, to await a better answer. Rizpah knew she would have to give them some reply. They were testing her. She had sought to restore unity, and now she was expected to propose a solution. *It's not fair,* she winced. *I didn't call this meeting. Why should they lay the burden of responsibility on my shoulders?*

She remembered similar words from Puah on the night her father died. "When you are ready to bear the burdens assigned to men, I will give heed to you," Puah had said. Could she bear this burden? Did she have the right to ask these men to give heed to her? As if on cue, the men all shifted again. Rizpah licked her upper lip. She hadn't much time to answer before they turned on her again, or worse, discarded her as useless.

Wringing her hands, Rizpah searched her mind, but her reeling thoughts were of the sorrow of being separated from her sisters by the Jordan. By the Jordan? If this was the fate of *her* family, why not...?

"I will tell you what I would have you to do." Rizpah nearly shouted in her haste to break the tension. "There is no reason those of us who want to take our inheritance in Canaan cannot do so. And—"

"Shall we take counsel from a woman?" Jair interrupted. "When an ass climbs a ladder, we may find wisdom in women. Give ear to *me,* my brethren, and I will tell you how to resolve our differences. Let us divide, but not in disharmony, only in location. You," he pointed to Hul, "shall have your inheritance in Canaan, and *we* will settle in Gilead," he finished, sneering at Rizpah.

The scene was as if Rizpah had never spoken; indeed, as if the women were no longer present. At first only a few men mumbled among themselves, slow nods moving their heads. Then, as the evening tide spreads upon the sands of shore, the nods extended to include all the leaders of Manasseh, accompanied by grunts and murmurs.

"Jair is right."

"Indeed, we don't all have to settle in Bashan."

"And we don't all need take our portion in Canaan."

"Hold, my brethren," cried Hul. "We cannot divide ourselves thus. We are one tribe."

"But if we try to force our preference on one another," Rizpah further explained the idea Jair had so artfully stolen from her, "we may end in war among ourselves. There is wisdom in *Jair's* counsel." She leveled a pointed gaze at Jair, who refused to meet her eyes. "It is true this is not the ideal solution, but when our inheritance is at stake, tribal loyalties can become clouded. If we are not content to be separated by only the Jordan, we could be divided by hatred."

Her words were again met with silent stares. She swallowed and looked to Mahlah for moral support. Had she spoken once too often? Would the men tire of interruptions and toss her out? To Rizpah's relief, Jair recalled the group's attention. "Most respected leader of Manasseh," he addressed Hanniel, "will you choose from among Manasseh's leaders upright men to go with you to Moses and speak of this matter, along with the men from Reuben and Gad?"

The slow tide of nods and murmurs swelled once more. Hanniel's left eye gravitated inward as his gaze drifted over the men's heads. He sighed and asked, "Is this truly what you wish?" Every man voiced agreement. "Then it is done, but the day grows late. I will choose the men tomorrow."

The men cheered, embracing and kissing one another on the cheek, smug in their renewed brotherhood. As the meeting broke up, talk once again turned to past and future victories of war. With a sigh of relief, mingled with exasperation that the men would not admit the solution (if it could be called that) had originated with her, Rizpah gave her sister a sidelong grin. Mahlah nodded in the direction behind her. Hul approached.

"Moses was wise to count you worthy to be heard, Rizpah." He kept his words curt and his eyes averted, but he was conceding her worth among the council. Before Rizpah could counter his greeting, he was gone.

As the men filed out, two more bowed to her in a grudging sign of respect before leaving. Basking in the spotlight of this meager, but nonetheless heady, acceptance, Rizpah was not aware that the room was empty until Hanniel stood before her.

His eyes sparkled as he looked down. "I will help you carry your sister home." He held out his hands and lifted Rizpah to her feet. She bent to reach for Mahlah's chair, but Hanniel held on to her. "Jair fooled no one by claiming your solution, save those who desire ignorance. But for your suggestion, the arguing could have dragged on until dawn. I am grateful for your wisdom." His raspy voice was even huskier than usual.

Rizpah nodded, her eyes captive to his, and tried to swallow past the constriction in her throat. "You are truly blessed among women, Rizpah. Someday I intend to write a song about you." Heat crept into her face. She stuttered her gratitude and dropped his hands. As she turned to Mahlah he added, "May your womb be blessed with many sons for Caleb." She knew without looking that the sparkle had left his eyes.

"Shall your countrymen go to war while you sit here?" Moses roared at the congregation of Gadites, Reubenites, and Manassites who had approached him with their request. The Tent of Meeting quivered with his response. "Why do you discourage the Israelites from going over into the land the Lord has given them? This is what your fathers did when I sent them from Kadesh Barnea to look over the land. The Lord's anger was aroused that day, and He swore they would not see the land He promised to Abraham, Isaac, and Jacob.

"And now, here you are, a brood of sinners standing in the place of your fathers and making the Lord even more angry with Israel. If you turn away from following Him, He will again leave all this people in the desert, and you will be the cause of their destruction."

Hanniel and the leaders of Gad and Reuben stepped forward. "Please, hear our people out," they beseeched Moses.

"Could any good come of this?" Moses' nostrils flared in rage, and his breath came as a charging bull as he roared, "Speak."

"Half of the tribe of Manasseh and all the people of Gad and Reuben seek to go build pens for our livestock, and to fortify the conquered cities for our women and children. We are also ready to then arm ourselves and go ahead of the Israelites into Canaan, until we have brought the Canaanites to their place. We will not return to our homes until every Israelite has received his inheritance. We will not receive any inheritance with them on the other side of the Jordan, save for the other half of Manasseh, because our inheritance has come to us on the east side of the Jordan, toward the sunrise."

Moses relaxed his stern countenance somewhat. "If you will do this—if you will arm yourselves before the Lord for battle, and if all of you will go armed over the Jordan before the Lord, until He has driven His enemies out before Him—then when the land is subdued, you may return and be free from your obligation to the Lord and to Israel. And this land will be your possession.

"But if you fail to do this, you will be sinning against the Lord God of Israel, and you may be sure your sin will find you out. Go first and build cities for your women and children, and pens for your flocks, but then return and do as you have promised."

The leaders of Gad and Reuben knelt before Moses along with Hanniel and said, "We your servants will do as our Lord commands."

After burying Mahlah's waste in the damp sand, Rizpah grabbed the emptied leather pail and spade and hurried from the stench of the area outside camp designated for the disposal of bodily waste. The unpleasant daily task thankfully completed, she sank to a large boulder, stealing a few moments of rare repose.

This time Rizpah did not hesitate to face the Ghor, looking full into the face of the future. Slipping off her sandals to bury her feet in the miniscule pebbles that made up the desert of the Moabite plain, she closed her eyes to absorb the warm tranquility of the azure sunset. The minor aches that plagued her hard-working, middle-aged body were massaged away by the rising breezes of evening that whispered promises of renewal.

Rubbing the small of her back, Rizpah felt a stab of guilt for being idle while Mahlah was left alone. Milcah spent her days with the flocks, and if Rizpah was busy, which she usually was, the time was lonely for Mahlah. Since all their family and friends had gone to settle before them in Gilead, the half-deserted section of camp left a gaping hole in their family security, and the three remaining women relied on one another for a sense of community.

Rizpah had urged that their little family be allowed to remain at Abel Shittim until Hoglah's and Tirzah's husbands had staked them a section of land in Gilead. With an invalid to care for, the three women could be of no real help there anyway. Mahlah had agreed with laughing eyes, but not before assuring Rizpah and Milcah she recognized their reasoning as nothing more than an excuse to stay and see Caleb and Othniel as long as possible.

Breathing in deep contentment, Rizpah flung a rain of sand upon herself with a joyous kick. *Nothing can pinion my heart now. I have the beginnings of respect from the men of my tribe, the future is settled for each member of my family, and I have an entire lifetime to love Caleb*. Wholly satisfied with the outcome of all her trials, Rizpah retrieved the leather bucket and returned home. *Surely Elohim is a just God. He is a rewarder of diligent seeking, and no one has sought a man's love more diligently than I*. A sharp sting of her conscience reminded her of Hanniel's steadfast love, and she shot to the Lord a guilty prayer for him to find a good wife. Rizpah even thought of offering a sacrifice for Hanniel's betrothal.

"I hope you weren't in need while I was gone," she greeted Mahlah as she hung the clean pail from a peg of the tent pole.

"Oh, but I wasn't alone."

Rizpah gathered the ingredients and utensils for Mahlah to cook supper. "Your eyes tell me it was not a visit from Aunt Puah that left them with that sparkle." She grinned as she bent to rekindle the cooking fire and watched Mahlah blush. "Why, sister, you act as a maiden again."

The first evidence of soft age lines outlined Mahlah's doe-brown eyes and her laugh brought attractive crinkles to her mouth. "Nathan was here. He asked me to marry him."

"*Mashallah!* What has God wrought?" Rizpah slapped the back of Mahlah's chair in glee. The contact reminded her of her sister's condition. Her eyes sobered. "He does not require you to—that is, to be a wife in every sense?"

"That is the first thing I asked him to consider. Rizpah," Mahlah grasped both her hands, "he doesn't care. He said I was as a balm to his lonely soul, and that was enough."

Rizpah hugged her sister tightly. "This is wonderful."

"Besides," Mahlah lowered her eyes. "Just because I cannot walk does not mean that Nathan cannot...know me." Rizpah stared. "Truly, Rizpah. I have thought of this often before. It is only my legs I cannot control. I have not much feeling, but it is not my enjoyment I am thinking of, anyway."

"Oh, my precious sister!" Rizpah cupped Mahlah's bright red cheeks. "Nathan will find much enjoyment with you, in *every* sense."

A scuffling at the tent opening drew the sisters from their embrace. A young boy panted, "Mistress Rizpah?"

"Yes?"

"Manasseh's leader sends you word to come to the Tent of Meeting at once. He says it is urgent."

The cool wind's earlier, promising caress whipped Rizpah's cheeks with stinging strands of hair as she sped on trembling legs in response to the summons. Her breath caught in short gulps, her wildly clenching fists grasping at the air with each stride, as if they could propel her forward. She kept her eye trained on the pillar of a cloud above the Tabernacle, miraculously transforming into a column of fire in the falling night, for it was evidence the Lord God wanted to speak to Moses. The symbol of Elohim's comforting presence was strangely ominous now. The setting sun threw a grim purple blanket over the Tabernacle as she arrived, panting. Inside, blinking in the shadows, she felt an arm reach for her. *Caleb*.

A hoarse voice grated near her ear. "I fear our uncle is at his mischief again."

Rizpah's heart fell when she realized she grasped Hanniel, and she released him. Her breathing came steadier now, and her eyes adjusted to the darkness. She could make out the forms of Salu and many other elders of Manasseh.

"Most exalted leader." Salu bowed low before Moses. "When Ha-Elohim commanded my lord to give the land as an inheritance to the Israelites by lot, He ordered you to give the inheritance of my brother, Zelophehad, to his daughters." Salu paused. Rizpah searched the room for Caleb and found him entering through the curtain with his comrade, Joshua, who was now officially appointed to lead Israel after Moses' death. She motioned to them, and Caleb was at her side immediately. Clutching his arm, she nodded toward Moses and Salu.

"Now, suppose..." Salu stroked his scraggly beard and dust rose from it. "Suppose they marry men from other Israelite tribes; then their land will be taken from our ancestral inheritance and added to that of the tribe they marry into."

Rizpah and Caleb stared at one another. The foreboding that had been building since Hanniel's summons crescendoed with a roar that nearly blocked out Salu's next words. From the depths of an echoing cavern, his words floated to her.

"And so, when the Year of Jubilee comes for the Israelites, the women's inheritance will be permanently added to that of the tribe they marry into."

The words registered in Rizpah's mind, but their impact drifted away on the echoes. Somehow she knew that if she relinquished the dreamlike state of shock, the words would assault her with a force she could not withstand. Moses stood. The movement was slow and weary, as if rubbery time had caught itself on an acacia limb and was stretched, until gradually all else slowed with it. Yet, time refused to stop, dragging relentlessly onward. The almost drunken slur of Moses' words in her ears were testimony of the pull.

"What the tribe of the descendants of Joseph says is right."

Time snapped. Rizpah felt herself hurled backward as if

slapped. Caleb's arm, supporting her, jerked as if he too felt the elastic sting of time catching itself. Moses glanced at Rizpah, but his sad gaze lingered on Caleb's face. The habitual fire within his eyes had died. Rizpah thought she had never seen the folds of his face so creased and ashen. She held her breath, awaiting his decree.

"This is what the Lord commands for Zelophehad's daughters. They may marry anyone they please..."

Rizpah almost squealed as she turned to embrace Caleb, but his stony countenance checked her action. She fell back as if stricken, at the rest of Moses' statement.

"...so long as they marry within the tribal clan of their father. No inheritance in Israel is to pass from tribe to tribe. Every daughter who inherits land must marry someone in her father's tribal clan."

Rizpah felt Caleb's arm tighten about her as Joshua embraced his friend in sympathy. Out of the corner of her eye she glimpsed Othniel hurrying from the Tabernacle, his face sullen, then Hanniel was before her. "I grieve for you, my cousin." His eyes included only her in his condolence. "If you have any needs, please allow *me* to fill them." His eyes flickered off Caleb as he stressed the word *me*. There was an expression in them Rizpah could not read.

Hanniel and Joshua disappeared in the crowd, and Rizpah looked up at Caleb through a haze of shock, to find him staring over the heads of the crowd of Israel's eminent leaders. She followed his gaze. His eyes were locked in the sorrow of Moses' stare. Caleb's eyes bored into Moses, as if to draw something from him other than the words he had just spoken. Moses lifted both hands in a shrug it seemed he could not complete for the weight of it. Then, with a slow shake of his head, Moses broke the gaze and left.

Joshua appeared and drew Caleb aside to inform him he would dismiss the men sorting weapons for him. A reptilian hiss chilled Rizpah's ear, and she brushed at it with her hand as she strained to hear Caleb's response to Joshua. Startled when the swipe brought her palm flat against someone's cheek, she shrank back. Salu's face reared before her.

"So." Her uncle squinted his eyes to mere slits, and in so doing brought the sickly yellow bags beneath them up to meet the scaly skin of his eyelids. "So, you sought to humiliate me before all the judges of the nation."

"No." Rizpah raised her hand in an effort to put some distance between them, but Salu bore down further.

"You little witch. I made sure you didn't get away with it, and I will make you my wife—or you'll curse the day you issued forth from your mother's womb."

"I will not marry you." Sudden, hot anger rose to Rizpah's cheeks. "You cannot force a marriage—"

"Silence." Salu raised his arm as if to strike her, then halted midair. He lowered his fist and rubbed it hard with his other hand. "Your uncles are your closest living relatives," he growled. "And I *will* have my way. No *woman,*" he spat after the word, "will stop me. You will marry *me* or no one." Her uncle twirled and stomped out of the Tabernacle when he saw Caleb approaching.

Rizpah clenched her fists convulsively, wishing with all her might that she could release some of her pent-up anguish with a hot bath of salty tears. None came, neither in the Tent of Meeting, nor during the numbing walk home.

When Rizpah and Caleb entered her tent the evening was late, but no lamps had been lit. Only the glow of the fire lit the room, and that was not enough to chase away the fearful shadows of a grim future. The only sound was the continual sobs of Milcah, muffled by Othniel's chest. As he held her Mahlah ladled sop into bowls and warmed loaves she knew no one would dip, but the activity filled the vacuum of loss. She pulled at Rizpah's sleeve. "You and Caleb go talk. There is nothing you can do here at the moment."

Gratitude flooded Rizpah as she bent to kiss her thoughtful sister. "Thank you. I could be of no comfort to Milcah anyway."

Mahlah patted her hand. "Go. You and Caleb, talk."

Rizpah nodded, and they left unnoticed. She followed Caleb wordlessly through the starlit night to the stream of Abel Shittim, and sat on the edge of a large boulder. The moon's silver reflection silhouetted Caleb as he stared into the water, his hands hidden by the sleeves of his robe as he clutched each wrist. The silence between them was thick, and Rizpah felt an urgency to shatter it.

"What will we do?" Her words sounded panic.

Caleb's response was wooden. "What *can* we do?"

"We can do *something*. There is always something we can do."

Caleb stared deeper into the water and shook his head.

Rizpah shouted at him. "Do not say no!"

"What else can I say? Elohim has spoken. His command is that we are not to marry."

"The Lord would not take you from me. I cannot lose you."

Caleb faced Rizpah and took her shoulders. "I too regret this—"

"Regret? Is that all? Do you have such control of your heart? Or is there no ache within it that bears controlling?" Rizpah's voice rose to a shrill, but then Caleb's look calmed her. His eyes revealed such agony that Rizpah melted into his arms in relief. "I thought for a moment you didn't love me. Oh, any ache but heartache." She rocked in his arms, but no tears would fall.

Caleb stroked her hair and whispered as if to himself. "I was wrong to ask you to marry me. I knew it then. This is my fault."

Rizpah lifted her head from his shoulder and grabbed his face between her hands. "That is not true. There is no wrong in the love between us." Searching Caleb's eyes, she found confusion there. "Caleb, you did no wrong. When you asked me to marry you, you fulfilled my life's dream. I have hoped since I was a child to become the wife of the noblest hero in Israel. I have always loved you. I always will." She pulled his forehead down to hers. "If there is any wrong here, it is mine. I practically begged you to marry me."

Caleb shook his head. "A woman like you need beg no man." He touched her cheek with his finger. "There is not a man among us worthy to be yours."

Ever so gently his lips brushed hers. She responded tenderly, as Caleb's breath came faster and his arms encircled her, his lips trembling as they crushed against her own. The lightning exploded behind her closed eyes with such blinding intensity that she didn't realize for a moment that Caleb had torn away and was again facing the stream.

"What?"

Shaking his head, Caleb's voice was strained. "It is no use. We must deny our feelings."

"I cannot."

"We must." Caleb whirled on her. His voice softened. "We cannot torture ourselves like this." He touched her lips with reverence. "I cannot bear another of your kisses. It would tear me asunder. Do you understand?"

"Yes," Rizpah whispered, still breathless. "But is there *nothing* we can do to alter—"

Caleb covered her mouth with his hand. Their eyes locked once more, and he pulled his hand away as if the touch had scorched him. Taking a step back, he said, "No, nothing. Elohim has spoken, and we must obey."

There was that thick silence between them again. Rizpah felt suffocated by it. *We must keep talking.* Words were all they had left, and when they were spent, it would be over.

Caleb cleared his throat. "This will probably be the last time we will see each other. The men from Gad and Rueben and Manasseh are due to return any day from building temporary cities for their families. You will be leaving soon." Rizpah nodded. Caleb paused, as if he too were hesitant to stop the flow of words, even if they were inane. "Your family should be safe within the protection they have erected. And

I...I am busy now, organizing the march into Canaan and drilling the troops."

Rizpah wrung her hands as he spoke. "We are marching much later than we had hoped. Already we begin the month of Nisan. It is well into spring." As if to verify the fact, he looked down into the slightly receding waters of the stream. Though it still was running briskly, by summer's end it would be merely a heavy trickle.

Rizpah could keep quiet no longer. She blurted, "Caleb, I shall die. Is there nothing—?"

"No!" he shouted. He turned to face her, and his eyes shone with tears. "No," he whispered. "There is nothing. Not anymore."

11

Hanniel stole quick glances at Rizpah pacing the sparse distance of the receiving section of her tent. He and Mahlah exchanged concerned looks as they shelled almonds for the almond and honey paste-buns Mahlah was preparing for their supper. "My eternal service is yours," he broke the tension, speaking to Mahlah, "for enduring my presence at yet another evening meal."

"Do not speak of it, my cousin. *Hadtha Beitak*—this is your house." Mahlah's answer was to Hanniel, but they both eyed Rizpah.

Hanniel could not help worrying over how peaked Rizpah had grown in the week since her betrothal to Caleb was broken off. His concern was such that he would have approached Moses about her state if their leader was in camp; but, at Elohim's request, Moses had ascended Mount Nebo, towering across the plain to the south. Though each evening most of Israel assembled outside camp to stand watch for his return, Hanniel thought they all sensed, as he did, that Moses would not return from this holy sojourn. The figure of Eleazer, the High Priest who had accompanied Moses, would trek back across the plain alone, ending their daily vigil and drawing a final curtain on an era.

"...and your company is always coveted here," Mahlah was saying to him.

The distant stare vanished from Hanniel's eyes with a bow of his head toward Mahlah. "You are too kind. I am ever your servant, and my tongue is your slave," he forced gaiety as he handed her his bowl of shelled almonds, "for I live for another of your paste-buns."

Mahlah's laugh was strained. "Ah, but Rizpah taught me how to make them."

"And what are you hiding from me, little cousin? I thought you could not cook."

Rizpah's response was to quicken her pace. Mahlah lifted her pestle at Rizpah's retreating back as if to speak, then, clamping her mouth shut, pulverized another mortar full of almonds. "You must be very lonely, with your sisters and their families all away at Gilead," she said to Hanniel at length.

"No more than I am sure you and Rizpah and Milcah are with your families gone. Where is Milcah?" Hanniel looked around and toward the door.

"She has taken the flock with another group of shepherdesses to more fertile ground, further north of camp. They take their evening meal together and strike out for home afterward. They seldom return before the moon is high."

Hanniel shifted. Conversation was awkward with Rizpah's pacing like a caged mountain lion. The swishing sound of Mahlah's whipping honey and goats' milk into the ground almonds momentarily drowned out the steady slap of Rizpah's thongs across the woven camel-hair rug. Mahlah snapped some twigs and dropped them into the fire within the clay jar-oven, then kneaded the dough one last time. "I am ready to bake the buns now, Rizpah. Would you stir the pottage? It smells like it's sticking."

No response. Mahlah heaved a sigh. Hanniel squatted beside the fire to stir the pottage, fanning the smoke away from him.

"I apologize." Mahlah indicated the stinging smoke and wiped sweat from her brow. "In this weather I should have cooked outside." Hanniel smiled and shrugged, and their eyes drifted back to follow Rizpah's shuffling form.

"I can bear this no longer," Rizpah blurted.

Mahlah set down the earthen cups she was arranging on the eating mat for their meal. She hefted herself in her chair and spoke as if resuming a conversation that had started before Hanniel arrived. "The pain would lessen if you would let go of your grief. Why do you hold on to it like this?"

Rizpah turned and strode the length of the tent again. "I must go see him." Hanniel ducked his head and stirred harder, feeling very much the intruder.

"But why?" Mahlah picked up a camel-hair pastry brush and spread the almond paste over the browned surface of the buns. "And why now, when we are ready to sup? We have a guest, you know."

Rizpah flounced to the floor before Mahlah. "Don't you understand? I can't bear this loss. Losing Father was grievous enough, but now..."

Mahlah stroked Rizpah's hair. The bronze wisps smoothed beneath her caress, and Hanniel's fingers ached to take the sister's place. "If you go to him, my sister, what will you say? Was it not all said before?"

Hanniel averted his eyes from the intimate scene, but in moments they were drawn again to the sisters, irresistibly. Rizpah closed her eyes tightly and inhaled. "I can no longer put off going to him. I see his face in my closed eyelids; I hear his breath in the breeze at my ear; I feel his touch with the covering of my bed—"

"Stop it, Rizpah. Why do you add to your pain?"

Rizpah's eyes snapped open. "Is it my pain you're concerned with, or do you tire of my complaints?"

Mahlah threw Hanniel a beseeching look, and he took her

part. "Come now, Rizpah." He stumbled over her name. "You cannot change a stubborn man's mind. Not even one of the brazen Midianite women could…I mean, not that you are brazen, only that…" Hanniel choked in confusion. He avoided Rizpah's quick look of surprise and, shrugging his helplessness to Mahlah, bowed again to his stirring. *I would not blame her if she threw me out after my idiotic blubbering. Can I never be of help to her in her need?*

"I beg you, do not go to him." Mahlah reached out to her sister, but Rizpah rose and stared down at her.

"I must."

Mahlah's face flushed. "Then hear me first. I have long admired your boldness, and I have been grateful to count you my mouthpiece before the council. I know you are quick and fearless when you see justice threatened. You are even chosen of God, as Father said on his deathbed. You were right about our inheritance, and you were wise to restore unity to Manasseh's council, but my Rizpah, you cannot *always* be right."

"I don't care to *always* be right, but this time I must."

"Elohim has ordered you not to marry Caleb." Rizpah flinched and turned her head as if to ward off an unseen blow. "Rizpah, there is a time when you must not fight, but surrender."

Hanniel gaped openly as Rizpah squatted once more before Mahlah with a tense and alert posture that pleaded for understanding. Her crimson and gold tunic cascaded in folds across the rug behind her as she grasped both Mahlah's hands. The broad, gold stripes of the dress flecked liquid drops of gold in her amber eyes, perhaps as a token for the teardrops Mahlah had confided to Hanniel that Rizpah was unable to shed.

"I have always fought," Rizpah said slowly, pumping Mahlah's hands with each barely audible word. "As a child I made Father and Mother see they were neglecting some of your needs, because they were needs that we supply ourselves without thought. I kept Father from being overly harsh with Milcah when he was afraid she would become vain because of her beauty. I have even fought for you when you were too timid to speak for yourself, but I have been content to be your mouthpiece. By all this I mean only to say, I have always had to fight."

"Yes, I know—" Mahlah said, her eyes sparkling with unspilled tears, but Rizpah continued.

"I fought Father to remain unmarried so I could wait for Caleb. That was a twenty-year battle." Hanniel winced, but Rizpah seemed to have forgotten his presence. "I even battled Caleb's own resistance to our age difference. Through all my years, the only battle that was for myself was for Caleb."

A lone tear squeezed from Mahlah's eye. "My heart bleeds for you in this, truly, but this prize you have set your determined eye upon is forbidden booty. Do you remember what Moses did when he saw that our army had taken the Moabite and Midianite women captive? He had every woman slain. Suppose you succeed this night in recapturing Caleb. What curse might you bring upon his head, and your own?"

"There will be no curse." Rizpah released Mahlah's hands. "Don't you yet see? There must be some mistake. Elohim would not reward my faithfulness by taking away the only thing I have asked for myself. He could not. I will find *something* Caleb and I can do."

"My dear, dear sister." Mahlah's face streamed with tears. "You have always found something to *do,* but—oh, how it tears my heart to repeat this—there is *nothing* you can do to alter this decree."

Rizpah's pale face was horror-stricken, and Hanniel thought the agony of her grief was more than he could bear. Then, the anguish seeped away, to be replaced by a forced serenity, willfully refusing to register the finality of the situation.

"You spoke to me of *right?*" Rizpah's voice was cold. "Is it *right* for Caleb to be taken from me? He whom I have saved myself for, whom I have loved these many years, whom I threw myself brazenly before, who has finally grown to return my love? I had to fight for our inheritance, and the respect of my tribesmen. And I will now fight for Caleb. He is rightfully mine!" Rizpah whirled and strode to the tent door.

Mahlah called after her. "You are correct that you fought for these things, but had our God not spoken through His servant Moses, the eyes of Israel would not have been opened to their injustice to women, and your efforts would have been in vain. Will it take Elohim speaking through Moses to open *your* eyes?"

Rizpah's back stiffened. Her anger burst full-blown as she stepped into the last moments of the exploding pinks and blues of sunset. Manasseh's grounds were on the westernmost side of camp, and since half the tribe had left for Gilead, the nearly deserted site posed no visual obstacles between Rizpah and the fiery ball plunging behind the fertile hills across the Jordan. The sun seemed to hasten to submerge itself in the cool waters of the Great Sea, beyond those fertile hills that formed the lower spine of Canaan.

In the brief moments she hesitated outside her tent, the sea indeed doused the radiance, and the cool breeze of nightfall rifled her hair, reminding her she'd forgotten her shawl. The brisk wind also served to temper her anger. A familiar, insistent voice reasoned within; her inherent trust in God argued with her will; but love for Caleb strove against them, piercing her heart with reminders of the touch of Caleb's lips on hers, fueling her grief with empty longings.

She struck out at a dauntless pace, eastward through the skeleton campsite where Gad and Reuben had been. At first relieved that the empty grounds meant no maze of tents and children and flocks to delay her, she soon discovered the abandoned expanse seemed to stretch infinitely before her, affording no measure of progress. With nothing to slow her advance, she found herself running by the time she crossed

Reuben, the easternmost edge of camp, and turned north through Zebulon. Her gait slowed to a long-legged lope through the densely populated grounds, and the strands of hair whipped loose by her pace straggled about her face. The crowds and the noise and the increased smoke from dinner fires barely penetrated her concentration, for as she entered Judah's camp and made her way to Caleb's home, she found it empty. A short, frantic search brought her to the Tabernacle.

Rizpah found Caleb behind the Tent of Meeting, sorting usable swords from those in need of repair. The sight of him brought the blood surging back to limbs that had seemed convinced they were dead. The sight of the weaponry quickly quieted her, however, as she was reminded that his departure was only a few days hence.

"Rizpah?" The concerned look on Caleb's face bore witness to her disheveled state. Quickly smoothing her hair and straightening her tunic, she went to him.

"I must talk with you." Her harried countenance bespoke the urgency.

Caleb's eyes swept the area where men counted and sorted the weapons, then scanned the sky. "Forgive me, men," he called. "I didn't realize the sun was gone. Go, and take supper. We will finish on the morrow." After the men left them alone, he pulled up a bundle of leather hides and seated Rizpah upon it. Facing her, he cleared his throat and waited.

Of a sudden, Rizpah was shy and at a loss for words. "What are these for?" She indicated the bundle of tanned hides, avoiding his gaze. There was only a quarter moon, and Rizpah was grateful that the heat of her face was hidden.

"For making shields." Caleb leaned closer, fingering one of the hides.

Why was it the moonlight, however faint, always spun his graying temple hair into webs of liquid silver? Her breath caught at his rugged attraction. "Caleb, my love—"

Caleb looked away so suddenly that she was startled. At her gasp, he closed his eyes tightly and sighed. Swift foreboding stole over Rizpah, warning her not to continue. Again the struggle lost to love. "Caleb, this week has been like a living death for me. I cannot—that is, don't you think—"

Caleb's laugh, too high-pitched, interrupted her. "I saw three sunrises without sleep. I had to beat the ground to keep Sheol from rising to engulf me alive. I paced the Tabernacle to demand if Elohim had deserted me."

"Then you feel as I do? It is not too late, Caleb. We can think of—"

Again he interrupted. "Yes, I felt as you."

His tone halted her. "Felt?"

"Listen to me, Rizpah."

She stood and backed away from him. "You *don't* feel as I do. I thought you loved me."

Caleb grabbed her arms to keep her from bolting. "Rizpah, you must give ear. Allow me the chance to explain." His voice was pleading. Rizpah swallowed and took a deep breath, her nails digging into her fists as she sat rigidly.

Caleb paced before her. "You mean so very much to me, so I want you to try to believe what I am saying. If we both do not accept this truth that I feel is from Elohim, we will grow bitter toward Him, and miss out on the promises of life." He paused. "You see, what we feel for each other was never love—"

Rizpah hurtled from the pile of leather, but she could not run. Her legs wobbled until she thought she would fall. The only way to remain standing was to lock her knees, keeping her back to Caleb.

Caleb hurried on, as if his voice would stay her. "At least, it is not the love for which we should marry. Please don't misunderstand, for I don't mean to detract from what we share. What we have is real, but it is not love. Think about it, Rizpah. You grew up hearing about the exploits of Joshua and Caleb. I was your hero because you admired the things

I'd done. And now I know why you admired me to such extent: because you are of the same spirit as I."

Rizpah shook her head. "No, you are so wise. . . ." Her voice was far off.

"And so are you, Rizpah. Use that wisdom to hear me. When was it that I claimed I loved you? When you stood with courage and wisdom against all the elders of the land. I recognized the spirit in you and mistook my admiration for love." He turned her around to face him. She tried to look at him, but the shock of his denial of love clouded the air between them.

"Not many people have the kind of fire within that you do, my Rizpah. It is your gift from God, and you have used it wisely for Him. There is not an honest man in Israel who does not respect you—and me, even more so. I will always care for you, perhaps more than for any person alive. Even were it not against God's command, we could not build a marriage on our great admiration for each other. Soon we would find a crack in the image we've constructed, and be disappointed. My little Rizpah, I could not bear to be disappointed in you."

The dark amber of Rizpah's eyes was barely visible behind her dilating pupils, growing wider with each denial from Caleb. The darkness about her pitched and rocked, as if she had boarded an unsinkable Phoenician ship. The ground swirled in misty eddies, as unfathomable as Caleb's words.

"All is not hopeless for us." Caleb's voice sifted through the rising mists and blew away some of their confusion. "We can look to the future. Moses told us before he left that in the promised land everyone will not do as he sees fit, as he does here. There will be no poor among us, for God will richly bless us in the land, if we fully obey Him."

A shudder convulsed Rizpah and wrenched the words from her throat. "I can never pretend I don't love you!" The moonlight paled her face to a ghostly white and tinged her trembling lips blue. "I trusted you with my love, and you returned it. I know you did. Why do you deny it?"

"Not deny it, Rizpah. Had the Lord not forbidden us to wed, I would still think I loved you in that way, but we both misinterpreted our feelings. We cannot go back—not now, not ever."

Rizpah stepped close, every taut muscle straining to make him love her again. "Hold me in your arms and kiss me, then tell me our love was a lie."

"Rizpah, I—" Caleb cleared his throat and stepped back. Rizpah tried to read the expression in his eyes, but the veil that forever protected them was tightly drawn, and she knew it would never part for her again. "I cannot. I must hold fast to what I've said until it becomes true in my heart. That is the only answer to my prayers. It must be enough."

Rizpah felt as if he'd spat upon her. "I am sorry, Caleb. It is not enough for me." Her words floated back to him on the breeze, for Rizpah had escaped into the night.

12

The partial moon's spectral lucency darted over tiny crevices that were already stretching the thirsty plain asunder with the late spring drought. Rizpah ignored the assistance the light offered to her path. *Home,* her determined thoughts urged her against the spurts of torchbearing countrymen headed outside camp to await news of Moses' mountain sojourn. *Home to Mahlah.*

A spectre of the former vibrant and indomitable Rizpah stumbled through the tent door to stand swaying and ashen-faced before the tent's lone occupant, Mahlah.

"*Mashallah!* Come to me, here beside me," Mahlah commanded immediately. She pulled Rizpah's head to her lap and stroked the fiery tresses that spilled over her knees. "Your hair has come unbound, my dove. Would you like me to comb it for you?"

Rizpah allowed her hair to be dressed, while she lay in Mahlah's lap, her dry, unseeing eyes propped opened in a deathly stare. "He doesn't love me."

"How could he not, my precious sister?"

"He said he never loved me."

"No, he didn't say that?"

"Yes."

Mahlah held Rizpah's head to

her breast, cooing. "Let your tears come, Rizpah. Holding on to them is like holding on to the grief. There is a cleansing in tears. Don't hold them back." Her words were soothing, but before either of them could give vent to their anguish, the tent door was slung aside with a whooshing sound. The women started.

Salu staggered across the room, his tangled black hair falling over bleary eyes. "So you would not marry me." He waved his arms wildly at Rizpah, his drunken words falling over themselves. "Do you think you are too righteous to be contaminated by my touch?" He reached a threatening, wine-stained hand toward her, but Rizpah scrambled to the back of the tent.

"I think you'd best leave," Mahlah ordered.

Rizpah's escape enraged him, and he lifted his face to the roof, bellowing like a bull. Lowering his head, he scanned the tent with bloodshot eyes until he spied Rizpah huddling in the corner. Fear was not foreign to her, but now terror rose in her chest, a new acquaintance, squeezing out even the ability to scream. Salu's hate-filled eyes stared through her as he lifted his sluggish feet slowly toward her, step by agonizing step. His breath was like that of a heaving elephant; his arms extended with clutching fingers scraping the air as he came.

Mahlah's breathing sounded somehow closer, and Rizpah chanced a glance in her direction. She gasped to see her invalid sister dragging herself across the floor, sallow cheeks puffing in and out with labored breath, fingers digging into the woven carpet; carpet that Rizpah remembered was embroidered by the very fingers that tore at it now. A thousand memories of Mahlah's unselfishness flashed through her mind as Salu followed Rizpah's stare. "You—leave—her—be—" The desperate invalid inched toward their uncle. "Get—out—get—out—"

Another animalistic roar issued from Salu's throat—or had she imagined it? *That's it. I must be dreaming. This is all a nightmare*. The reality of Salu, towering over the cripple, convinced Rizpah of her error. "O my God, my salvation! No!" Her scream did nothing to prevent the heavy wooden bowl's hurtling from Salu's upraised hands and crashing to Mahlah's head, nor did it stay the gush of blood spurting over her sister's closed eyes.

Salu tottered victoriously over the crumpled body, then howled as Rizpah lunged for his eyes with her fingernails.

"You son of Baal!" she cried hysterically. "If you've killed her I'll—"

One slap of Salu's hand sent her flying across the tent. She had no idea a drunken old man could be capable of such power. She landed on her back, and before she could scramble up, Salu was atop her. His face loomed above her in loathsome detail, blocking all else from sight. All she could take in was the dirt, the sticky, dried wine, the yellowish bags beneath his eyes and the green, reptile-like skin of his eyelids, his unruly beard filled with dust and sand, and all of it streaked with sweat and wine and smelling of mildew.

Rizpah turned her face and struggled to free herself, but the dead weight of a drunk was too much for her. "So, you would not marry me?" he repeated, the stench of his hot, sour breath filling her nostrils. "And now I have fixed it so you will not marry Caleb, haven't I?" His shrill laugh nearly deafened her, leaving her ears ringing with a nightmarish shattering of her senses. "Haven't I? You little witch! After tonight, *no* man will ever marry you."

His clumsy hands fumbled until he clasped the neck of her tunic, and with a screech that she couldn't be sure came from his throat or the rip of material, he tore her dress to the waist. The stupefying realization of his intentions paralyzed Rizpah, as she felt his hands reaching beneath her tunic. "My God, my rock, cover me with Your protection," she whimpered, closing her eyes.

"Cover you?" Salu's mocking laughter pealed. "I'll *uncover* you."

A rush of cold air slapped against her bare legs, reviving a last surge of strength, which she used to scream so loud and long she wondered if she only imagined it. She held the scream, knowing the impact of Salu's body falling atop her again would force the air from her lungs, claiming her last defense. Then she remembered there was no one to hear. The few that remained were awaiting Moses outside camp. Was she still screaming, or were her ears only ringing? Was she still conscious? What was the use? There was no one, no one; all was lost. Mahlah was dead, her purity would be defiled, camp was empty, Caleb didn't love her.

There was to be no blessed escape into unconsciousness, for Salu shook her—she supposed to deny her the mercy of being unaware what was about to happen to her. She realized she was still screaming, her lungs on fire. Salu shook her again, and she screamed louder, and then soft, warm lips were kissing her cheeks, her forehead, her closed eyes. She drew an incredulous breath.

"My love, my love! It's all right. It's me. Shhh." *Is Salu trying to trick me? No!* She would not give in to him without a fight. Blindly she clawed at him, kicked and bit and drew another burning breath to scream, but the strength was gone and she fell limp.

Hands stroked her hair and lips kissed her face, and Rizpah sucked in one more breath to heave a scream that came out as only a long, catching moan. Then those lips were over hers. She squirmed to escape, but to no avail. The fight was out of her. Come what may, she could only pray for death to take her. But those lips were lingering on hers, soft and warm and moving as if they were trembling, and she knew they were not Salu's.

Her eyes opened to the fuzzy russet of thick wavy hair. Relief flooded her with such force she was left more helpless than with her terror. With an inexplicable stirring within—not lightning bolts, but a whisper of some elusive, peaceful emotion—she found herself responding to Hanniel's kiss. *Not Hanniel. He cannot make me feel like this, only Caleb can*...but Caleb didn't love her and now here was Hanniel....

"Mahlah!" she whispered against his lips. Then louder, "Mahlah!" She struggled to raise up, but Hanniel held her.

"She is all right—all right. Can you understand me, Rizpah? I have taken care of her. She has been knocked out, but she is alive, and she will be conscious soon. She is well." Finally the words sank in and Rizpah collapsed again into Hanniel's arms, limp and lifeless. With thick, stubby fingers, Hanniel prudently situated the folds of her torn tunic to cover her and pulled her closer. "It's all over now."

Rizpah's blank gaze registered on the slumped body of Salu, and she gasped. Blood gushed from his belly. "Do not fear him," Hanniel soothed. "He can not hurt you now. He is dead." Rizpah lifted widened eyes to him. "I am sorry I have made you unclean by touching you when I have killed a man." Hanniel's voice tightened. "He fought like a wounded lion. He had a knife—his hands were clumsy—I tore it from him and...and then you needed me."

Hanniel tilted her face up to his and gently brushed her lips with his. Every muscle and sinew of her being arched to receive his kiss, buoying her on a pink drifting cloud, tossed about by lazy breezes that bade her reside in his arms indefinitely. Slowly, unobtrusively, the breeze stiffened, sighing in the wake of rising passion, pushing her harder and faster than she wanted—especially since she knew not *what* she wanted.

The first sob was muffled by Hanniel's lips, and the next and the next by his chest, where he held fast her head while her body shook with ever increasing sobs, until she heaved with the tears that had for so long refused to fall, and now expelled themselves with violence. Long before the last sob racked her body, her stomach ached with the involuntary convulsions, and all the while, Hanniel rocked her and kissed her head, wiping the torrent of tears from her face as fast as they came.

"I remember," Rizpah gasped between sobs. "My father

said I would stand for justice, and justice would circumcise me. I once thought that was fulfilled in my trials, but now I am truly cut off—cut off from life." She looked up into Hanniel's eyes and moaned, "Is this justice?"—and was shocked into silence to see his own ruddy cheeks streaked with tears.

An eerie moan drifted into the tent from a great distance, its familiar, high-pitched cadence drawing their attention. "Could that be . . . ?" Hanniel's voice was hushed and he hesitated, listening.

The wail increased, thousands of voices rising to match its timbre, until a lone voice was heard above them. "Rend your garments, O Israel! Let ashes cover your heads, for our mighty leader, Moses, has gone the way of all the earth."

A hoarse moan escaped Rizpah's raw throat. What more could she bear? Her life was torn in tattered pieces all about. Her eyes wandered over the shambles of the tent. Spades and ladles and broken pottery were strewn across the floor from her battle with Salu. The unconscious form of Mahlah lay near the center, the lethal wooden bowl overturned beside her, and beyond her the slumped figure of Salu, his blood finally emptied into a still puddle under his belly. And Caleb . . . he might as well be dead also, as dead as she felt.

The tent was suffused with death. The past was dead, and the future? For Rizpah, there was none. Yet, why did a golden thread of hope seem to flutter before her, making jabbing attempts to mend two pieces of her torn life, whose colors clashed and whose material was obviously of an incompatible weave.

Rizpah did not know how long she lay huddled in Hanniel's arms while he slowly rocked her, stroking her hair, until sleep finally came. She dreamed of the golden thread, still making attempts at joining the two unlikely cloths of her life.

13

An early morning mist hovered over the river Jordan, parting with a disconcerting clarity as it wafted heavenward. Hanniel watched Joshua stride across the misty eastern shore where Israel broke their three-day camp, shedding the fog like some deity throwing off the mantle of the natural. He thought Joshua blended too easily with the uncanny scene.

While waiting for the rest of his countrymen to finish breaking camp, Hanniel whittled. Clearing the middle hole in the reed flute he had designed, he felt pricks of some indefinable something raise the hairs of his neck—something he sensed had to do with the hovering mist.

Shifting position against the rock where he leaned for support, he attributed the phenomenon to the chill of dawn in the face of the coming heat, and eyed the flute's crude mouthpiece. Satisfied with its shape, he tested the pipe with a jaunty shepherd's tune. His neighbors responded with appreciative looks and waves, even a few dance steps around their packed camels and mules.

The huge camp scurried around him in the haste to move out, their constant movement snake-like upon the desert shore. Feeling isolated from the activity, Hanniel blew a lonely, piercing melody, and his heart burned with the absence of Rizpah. Warmth crept up his arms at the memory of holding her to his chest. Had that evening been only a week ago? His lips trembled at the thought of their kiss. *I know she responded to me,* he determined for the hundredth time. *But if that is true why has she ignored me since that night?* She had not even said good-bye when she left for Gilead.

He felt as if they were reliving the days when their only contact had been through Zelophehad, relaying Hanniel's proposals and Rizpah's refusals. He'd lived with a loneliness during those times that was stayed only by the hope that they would marry. This new aching, however, had grown more intense since his contact with her had become personal, and it was very nearly more than he could bear.

Nor could he bear much longer the forcefulness of God's presence that he had felt this morning. In fact, since the spies had returned from Jericho a steady anticipation of the wondrous had mounted. Some of that awe had come on the night so many years ago when he felt God promised him he was to wed Rizpah. Now, he was experiencing the same fearful excitement he'd known twenty years ago.

Hanniel attempted to sort and order his emotions concerning Rizpah logically, to separate past from present, but his mind meshed them together. With each passing year the assurance that the Lord had given this promise waned; yet each year he waited for Rizpah. Though she had thoroughly rejected him, the longer she remained unwed, and now that he'd experienced protecting her and had tasted of her lips, the stronger grew his love and determination to marry her.

In an attempt to push his confusion aside, Hanniel situated his stocky legs around the boulder and practiced another tune. The burdened camels snorted behind him. He continued to watch Joshua finalize the breaking of camp, wondering what their leader had in mind. The Jordan was at flood stage, so fording was out of the question. The only hint

Joshua had given them was last night, when he said they were all to consecrate themselves before the Lord—the usual practice before going to war.

Hanniel mulled the puzzle over as he, along with the tribes of Gad and Reuben, stared stupidly at the rushing waters before him. Their three tribes were assembled first, for they would march armed before the rest of Israel, as Moses commanded them. Fingering the sword at his side, Hanniel tapped the upturned flute against the boulder to clear it.

Joshua strode toward the Levites surrounding the ark and shouted, "Take up the ark of the Lord and go stand in the river."

The priests obeyed without hesitation, their brief glances at one another the only betrayal of their bewilderment. Their steps were halting, though, as they made their way along the swampy shore, taking great care to balance their treasure. The golden ark sparkled reflections of the heavens into the purpled depths of the river, sparking expectations among God's people with sunlit beams that shot over their heads as in blessing.

Turning to face the throng of Israelites, Joshua lifted his arms. "Come, listen to the words of the Lord your God. This is how you will know that Elohim the living God, is among you, and that He will certainly drive out before you all the nations of Canaan. See, the ark of the Lord of all the earth will go into the Jordan ahead of you. As soon as the priests who carry the ark of the Lord set foot in the Jordan, the water flowing downstream will be cut off and stand up in a heap."

Waves of incredulous gasps washed over the nation as the priests ventured the first tremulous step into the swirling waters. The foam vanished from the river's surface as the rushing became a mere flow. "Look!" A cry arose and every eye turned upstream. It was as if the water were the sedentary substance and the dry ground came gushing downstream to flood it with earth. Hanniel's head swiveled as the tide of soil sped past them to disappear into the salt sea region of the Arabah, swallowing the river as it went.

The priests carried the ark to the middle of the Jordan and waited, but they turned to see not a commencing march, but their countrymen, every one, upon their knees, a glorious babble of praise rising like incense heavenward. Hanniel's mouth went dry before he realized it hung agape at the wonder. His reverent silence erupted into adoration for his God. As far as the eye could see, in either direction, no water could be found. He scanned the earthen riverbed until Joshua's command to cross rang out.

Springing from his rock, he stuffed the flute into his girdle as Manasseh, Gad, and Reuben moved out first. His throaty voice mingled with his tribesmen and the women and children as they joined in a rousing marching song.

> Elohim Hayyim is among His people.
> The land across the Jordan will cower,
> As whipped dogs they shall cower before us.
> The One True God will drive them from the land,
> The land He has given to Israel.

Stepping into the riverbed, Hanniel was amazed that only the banks held the muddy moisture that evidenced water. Scraping the soles of his sandals upon the dry riverbed, each step gave rise to an emotion that threatened to take his breath away. Truly, he doubted that he breathed until his soles squished in the mud of the west shore. The singing crescendoed with a deafening roar. *Perhaps to replace the roar of the Jordan,* Hanniel thought as the last of the Israelites emerged from the riverbed.

A torrent of thoughts crashed against a mighty dam of revelation that bound past to present. Hanniel now marched in fulfillment of a forty-year-old promise. The same God that had promised him Rizpah twenty years ago, hovered over the waters today. With finality, Hanniel knew he would soon be Rizpah's husband.

The morning coolness had long since dissipated, and the heat bore down with a rhythm matching their victory call stroke for stroke. The ark radiated power from the river's center, and through the almost visible waves came their leader's voice.

"Choose twelve men from among the people, one from each tribe, and tell them to take up twelve stones from the middle of the Jordan, from where the priests stand, and carry them back to the shore."

Hanniel agreed as the tribal elders almost unanimously chose Hul as Manasseh's representative. Hul joined the eleven other men, and the twelve moved as one unit to retrieve the boulders from the earth.

"Carry these stones with you to the place where we will camp tonight," Joshua instructed. "There we will set them up. And in the future, when your children ask you, 'What do these stones mean?' tell them that the flow of the Jordan was cut off before the ark of the covenant of the Lord when it crossed over. Tell them these stones are a memorial to the people of Israel forever. May all the earth praise His holy name!"

The Levites left their place amid the Jordan, and as soon as the last foot retreated from the riverbed the sound of rushing waters roared from a distance, the wall of noise breaking over them nearly as crushing as the tide of the Jordan replenishing itself. Where there was no water, it now rushed again at flood tide.

Hanniel stared deep into the swirling, foaming waters, as the Jordan again washed its shores before him. *What a picture of the glory of the trustworthy Elohim!* The power of his Lord exploded inside him, bathing him in its tide with peace and fulfillment.

Hanniel's breath came in deep, wheezing gasps as he scrambled between massive limestones hewn from the rock quarry on the slopes south of the city of Ai. Perspiration drenched him, stinging the legion of cuts and bruises covering his legs and arms. The cry of retreat stalked him as he wedged aching shoulders into the crevice between limestone pillars, sliding his arms into the narrow strips cut behind them on either side. His hand brushed a workman's pick still lodged in the earth, left for convenience's sake when the workman would return. His breath rasping in his heaving chest, Hanniel examined the instrument. His sword had been lost in the vain battle at Ai, where he'd been separated from his troop. This pickax was a poor substitute for the weapon, but it was all he had.

A sprinkle of loose dirt from overhead pelted his feet. Hanniel's heart melted and became like water as he held his breath, his lungs bursting from his desperate race for the slopes. He was fortunate to have stumbled into the quarry where there were so many places to hide from Ai's soldiers, who may even now hover over him.

Flattening into the dugout, he glanced up at the mud and rock overhang. His hideout sheltered him from view above and to the left and right. The only place from which he could be spotted was straight ahead, and in order to reach him one would have to travel through a pass of limestone rubble about five feet below and then double back to where the pass dropped off to his left. Hanniel would be able to spy anyone in the pass before they had the chance to round the boulders and attack.

With no other evidence of movement above, Hanniel relaxed slightly to absorb the damp coolness of earth and rock, but kept a grip on the pick. His leather breastplate stuck to him through the camel hair tunic. His sweat-plastered hair, whitened from a dusting of the alkaline residue of limestone, matted in the mud at his back. A thousand questions ran through his mind—or was it really only one question, echoing repeatedly in imitation of the sun's glare, bouncing off the hundreds of white boulders: *What happened?*

Where was the protection and victory Moses and Joshua

had assured them of? Flashes of the miraculous parting of the Jordan and the glorious destruction of the walls of Jericho rose to taunt him. With all Elohim had done for them, would He desert them now? *What had gone wrong?* How could Israel be reduced from devouring victors, holy warriors of Elohim, into cowering shadows retreating from the small city of Ai like a band of marauding thieves? Ai was so insignificant compared to Jericho that their spies had advised them to send only three thousand men to battle. Now, the three thousand ran like jackals, and Hanniel hid as a timid rock partridge.

At the sudden scrape of feet below him, Hanniel gave his wet palm a quick swipe against his tunic and edged into a position to observe the pass. His head throbbed with the pounding of his heart, but the intruder proved to be his cousin Ludim, Hoglah's husband, who scurried alone into the pass, tossing furtive looks behind him. Before Hanniel could signal, a blur of flesh and metal and leather pounced from above, two soldiers of Ai landing in front of Ludim, laughing, their swords dancing before him in the sunlight.

With a thrust of his legs Hanniel landed behind them. The soldiers whirled in confusion at the thwarted ambush, giving Ludim time to appraise the odds and draw his own sword. The moment hung suspended in time. All eyes were on the pick Hanniel waved heroically.

"I h-hope you don't mind my balancing the s-scales." His stuttering statement sounded ridiculous even in his own ears.

The two enemy warriors glanced at each other and smiled. Ludim's face paled. Hanniel's knees wobbled as he too stared at the ludicrous defense he held. At least the element of surprise had given Ludim a fighting chance. *Now, what of my own chances?* Hanniel gulped.

Still smiling, the warriors of Ai poised back to back for battle, assurance of victory gleaming in their eyes. Hanniel thrust his pick at the soldier facing him.

"We fight in the name of Elohim, the one true God," he boasted.

His opponent threw his head back in laughter, parrying Hanniel's thrusts with terrifying ease, then brought his head down with a deadly stare, his eyes as sharp and cold as the metal he gripped. Slowly he pointed his sword at Hanniel. His eyes narrowed and he lunged on one bent leg, thrusting the huge, wide blade with the sickening clink of metals connecting. Hanniel brandished his short ax blade, but each clanging whack backed him further from Ludim's desperate struggle, and closer to the short drop-off at the turn in the pass.

Their frantic shuffling stirred up clouds of dust and limestone chalk, stinging their eyes and forcing choked coughs between grunts and thrusts. The few offensive stabs Hanniel attempted brought a chilling gurgle from his enemy's throat that he barely recognized as laughter. With a quick glance over his shoulder, Hanniel surveyed the short, sharp drop-off behind him, his chances of survival looming increasingly slim.

Defeat was inescapable, unless he could find another weapon. Miraculously, he had stayed his opponent as long as he had. Then a sharp, jutting stone in the quarry bed below offered hope. Dodging a last thrust from the sword, Hanniel pretended to lose balance and tumbled off the pass's edge, twisting in midair. He cushioned the fall with a roll toward the jagged rock, directing himself so that it would appear his head had smashed fatally into it.

His direction was off, and his ear thwacked the protuberance harder than planned. Lying motionless and bleeding, he held his breath, praying the soldier would think him dead. Hearing the scrape of the unconvinced soldier's feet stumble down the steep slope, Hanniel nearly bolted. The blood oozing down his face might yet fool his enemy.

The soldier kicked Hanniel's legs and side unmercifully, and it took every bit of will power Hanniel had not to cry out.

Then there was silence. Hanniel dared to hope his attacker had gone, but something in the silence warned him the soldier's sword was raised high, poised to complete the victory. His heart lurched, and he tensed to roll quickly when a shout came from above.

Dirt and pebbles flew all around him as the enemy turned and scrambled to join his comrade. Hanniel watched him disappear over the pass's edge; then he jumped to his feet, wincing with the pain of the beating, and followed as quietly as possible. He knew surprise was his only remaining weapon, but with it he might save Ludim.

Mounting the slope, hidden by a large limestone pillar, Hanniel crept past the backs of the enemy. Ludim was pinned against the rocky hillside, grunting and wheezing in futile defense. Quickly Hanniel climbed to his earlier perch, planning to swoop down upon them, but before he could reach the ledge a scream froze his stride. Laughter filtered up to him and Hanniel knew it was too late. Congratulatory slaps and shouts stung his ears as he squirmed to the edge of the overhang. As soon as the soldiers were clear of the quarry, Hanniel dropped the five feet to where his cousin lay. Ludim's eyes still stared in horrified understanding of his fate, and *blinked*!

"Ludim!" Hanniel knelt and grabbed his shoulders. "You live!"

"Hanniel..." Ludim's voice mingled with a gurgle that sent shivers up Hanniel's spine. "Hoglah...my daughters...will you...they need...she needs..."

"Shhh." Hanniel brushed the hair from Ludim's face. "Do not worry about your family. They are my family too. I will care for them. They shall want for nothing as long as I live."

Ludim coughed and a stream of blood seeped from the corner of his mouth. "Hoglah is...she is not the pillar of strength she appears. She...she needs more than the care you speak of. Hanniel, she needs a man...a husband." The emphasis Ludim put on the last word sent him into spasms of coughing that Hanniel could do nothing to ease. He could only hold Ludim tightly, cushioning his back from the rocky ground. When the fit subsided Ludim's face was the color of the chalky limestone, and his voice barely audible. "Hanniel, you must marry her."

"Ludim!" Hanniel nearly dropped him. "You don't know what—"

"Will you wait another twenty years for her?"

Hanniel said nothing.

"Hanniel!" Ludim breathed softly, but with passion. "Marry Hoglah. I have no brother to take her. You are my cousin...a good man...I trust you."

"I cannot. You must not ask me."

"But I ask. Grant me this dying request."

Hanniel knew the torment his cousin bore, knowing his wife and children would be left desolate. "I promise you, I will care for them until I die."

"Marry my wife so that I may go to my fathers in peace. I cannot rest knowing that Hoglah is alone—" Coughs overtook Ludim again and Hanniel held him securely. Ludim recovered faster this time, only to slip into near-unconsciousness. "Do not deny me," he whispered, his lips barely moving.

"How can you ask this of me? How can you expect me to give up Rizpah?"

"You never had Rizpah," Ludim murmured, his eyes closed now. "But you have Hoglah. I give her to you. Please, I beg you."

"I—"

"Promise me you will marry her."

"But—"

"Promise!"

Hanniel was silent.

"Hanniel, give me your word!"

Hanniel could only understand Ludim's last command by reading his lips, for the breath of life ebbed away and he held a dead man in his arms. Sobbing like a child, he rocked the corpse for long minutes. Again, words had failed him when he needed them most. One word would have sufficed: *yes*.

Hanniel stood and looked at his cousin. Anger at the fate that thwarted him at every turn swelled. He raised his fist to the sky, screaming, "You had no right, Ludim. You had no right to lay the burden of this request on me." He tore at his hair. "Now you make me bear the guilt of refusing your dying wish." Smothering his agony in the dirt, Hanniel fell on his face, and there he remained.

When frustration gave way to mourning, he rose to the task of burying Ludim, his own bruised and battered form nearly collapsing under the weight of the body. Finding an appropriate cave in these foothills was time-consuming, but the diversion of burial gave vent to rational thinking. Hanniel struggled to pile the last rocks in front of the tomb's entrance after laying Ludim's body inside and leaned against them.

"So be it, my cousin. It will be as you wish." Hanniel staggered toward the camp at Gilgal, his hope of marrying Rizpah entombed in the cave with Ludim.

14

Hanniel groaned in his sleep and eased onto his side, pain searing every muscle. He lifted one heavy eyelid. *Where am I?* was his first thought. Soft, wooly blackness entombed him, save for a darting, silver sliver at his feet. He strove for his last conscious memory. Last night he had stumbled into Gilgal, the warm safety of the campfires leading him as he crawled the last hundred yards. It seemed dozens of hands had grabbed for him, and at first his clouded mind could not register if the hands had reached to help or to harm.

Memory of yesterday's ambush rushed back. *Ludim is dead.* Hanniel reached leaden hands to cover his face as fresh tears constricted his throat, ripping at its parched, dust-coated lining. The silver sliver at his feet rippled fluidly, and a gust of cool, damp air lifted the hairs on his shins like hundreds of caterpillars crawling up his legs. The blackness around him brightened long enough for him to glimpse something smooth and tubular poised upright at his side. *A striking serpent!*

Hanniel jerked sideways and rolled to a sitting position. As he did so his foot touched the silver sliver, enlarging it until the inside of his small tent was filled with the sunlight from its foot-drawn opening. The striking serpent was only a sturdy tent pole.

A hand drew the tent flap aside further and fastened it, so that the early morning sun exploded over a disoriented Hanniel. A large form darkened the doorway, bending to look in at him.

"I see you have recovered," an unmistakable slow, thoughtful voice rumbled. Caleb lowered himself into the small tent and sat cross-legged, as Hanniel realized the buzzing in his head was the noise of a crowd gathering outside. Caleb held out a bowl of broth and a crusty barley loaf, which Hanniel accepted gratefully. He hadn't eaten since the morning before—before they attacked Ai.

After wolfing down the breakfast, he spoke. "How many died?"

"Over thirty that we know of."

Hanniel sighed and wiped the bowl clean with the last morsel of bread before setting it down. The two men stared at one another. "My cousin is among them."

"I know." Caleb's gaze was steady. "That was all you could say when we dragged you to your tent last night."

Again silence hung between them. Caleb cleared his throat. If Hanniel could not marry Rizpah now, there were some things he had to know. His left eye crossed slightly in concentration, and his gruff voice was low.

"I have long wanted to ask you something. Now seems to be time." Caleb nodded for him to continue. "How could you put Rizpah through it?"

"You are very angry with me, aren't you?" Caleb asked. Hanniel dipped his chin in a slow nod. Caleb cleared his throat. "It was never my intention to hurt her."

"But how could you have intended otherwise?" Hanniel exploded. "You had to know that everyone in camp heard of the words Zelophehad spoke on his deathbed. Ignoring his plea was a direct rejection of Rizpah. How could you do that to her?"

"I owe you no explanation."

"You do if your claim to love her was ever true."

For a moment their iron wills battled in silence, until the curtain in Caleb's eyes was drawn aside. With a sigh, he lowered his gaze. "I had to be sure of my feelings for her." His tone was defensive as he laced his fingers together around his knee. "That first night when she declared her love to me," he paused, "it was as if she were *defying* me to respond." He looked back up at Hanniel. "It was all I could do to keep from taking up her challenge."

"Then why—"

"I have never been one to make rash decisions." Caleb's voice was too loud, too harsh. "It took me five years to decide to marry my wife—but there is something about Rizpah." His voice softened and he laughed. "No one has ever before tempted me to act before I think. There are not many women like her." Caleb searched Hanniel's stony face as if pleading with him to understand.

But Hanniel was insistent. "Then why did you not let her know these things from the beginning? She suffered much shame among her neighbors. And then her uncle...you could have prevented his treachery if you had been honest with Rizpah."

"I have been without a woman for nineteen years. As I said, I wanted to be sure of my feelings. My reaction could have been...yearning." Caleb held up a hand as Hanniel opened his mouth to argue. "I know that sounds like a feeble excuse to you, but you must remember: you have been sure of your love for twenty years. It was sprung on me like a lion falling into a trap.

"And indeed, I felt trapped. You think I was not aware of Rizpah's situation, of the rumors she had to endure? All of that made me feel pressured to make a decision. I have learned that decisions made under pressure are as reliable as a crooked arrow. In all fairness to Rizpah, I had to be sure if I loved her or desired her, or if I merely sought to spare her from humiliation. Which is the more loving, to force her to live with a man who doesn't love her, or allow her to suffer the present pain, which will pass, and spare her an unfulfilled marriage?"

"Then you didn't love her?"

Caleb sighed. "I didn't say that. I said I refrained until I could make sure I loved her."

"And then you were sure, so you asked her to marry you?"

Caleb nodded.

"And then, after God commanded the two of you not to marry, you realized you had only thought you loved her?"

Caleb hesitated at how ridiculous Hanniel's summation made it sound, but he cleared his throat and gave a quick nod.

Hanniel smiled. "I understand."

"You do?"

"I *understand* how loving Rizpah can make sensible men run in circles as a dog chasing its tail."

Caleb's slow grin spread over his face as the two men laughed at themselves. Hanniel then peered at Caleb. "Is it true then? Have you learned that you never loved her?"

Caleb sobered. Again he laced his fingers over his right knee. "A man who does not keep his passions under control is no man. You know yourself the emotions Rizpah evokes." He paused as if to sample those emotions. "But, for some reason, Elohim has decreed that we shall not unite." Caleb's fingers clenched. "I don't know for certain that I never..." The older man swallowed. "Don't you see? If I am to keep my...if I am to obey the...at least for now, I *must* believe that I never..."

Hanniel broke the silence of the words left unsaid. "I have long blamed you for Rizpah's troubles." Caleb looked at him sharply. "First, because you refused to declare your love, and then because you did. If Rizpah had never become involved with you, she would not have had to defy her uncle before the council because she wanted to marry you, and then Salu would not have brought the case against heiresses marrying outside their own tribe."

Caleb cleared his throat. "If Rizpah had never become involved with me, there would be no heiresses." Hanniel narrowed his eyes. Caleb's tone changed. "And then again, if you had married her years ago, none of this would have happened."

Hanniel's husky voice caught as he thrust his fingers into his hair. "If I had been man enough to make her love me, she would have been spared all of this."

Caleb shook his head. "I said that only so you will understand how everything has happened according to Elohim's will. None of us are to blame. All of us are only stumbling along the best we can."

Hanniel looked at Caleb with slightly cross-eyed thoughtfulness. Recollections of the past flashed through his mind as he mulled over the truth of Caleb's words, and then he spoke. "You are not my enemy."

Caleb smiled and held out his hand. "I am your brother." They clasped hands, and Caleb added, "I am on your side in keeping our Rizpah from being hurt, but no one can stand in the way of Elohim's will directing their lives."

Hanniel was appeased. Somehow, Caleb's suffering atoned for Rizpah's. Still, to what purpose were their tangled lives?

The buzz of voices had grown loud enough to attract the two men's attention. Caleb gestured outside. "Joshua has called a meeting. I came to see if you were rested enough to attend."

"Of course." Hanniel rose and gripped his bruised side with a painful grimace.

Caleb steadied him. "Hanniel, do you remember that I once said to you, 'A man is known by his anger'? I spoke true. When I saw how angry you were at me for neglecting Rizpah, I knew your heart was honorable." He paused. "A man like that I can entrust her to. *That* is why I came to your tent."

Caleb's reassurance was lost in the despair that overwhelmed Hanniel as he remembered his promise to Ludim. Caleb was right. No one can stand in the way of Elohim's will, and it seemed at every turn he was blocked from Rizpah. What *was* right? Could he have been so wrong these many years? Squaring his shoulders against the day, Hanniel stepped outside just as Joshua began to address the troops.

He squinted in the sun's glare and quickly found a place in the crowd where he could see their leader. Joshua lowered the arms he had raised to call his army to attention. "I spent last evening on my face before the ark of the Lord." Joshua spoke in a normal tone, but the words vibrated like ominous thunder over the men. "The priests and elders of Israel prayed also. We had to know why Elohim has removed His blessing from His people." He paused, then began a fierce pacing, agitating a cloud of dust around his feet.

"I cried out in the temple, 'O sovereign Lord, why did you bring this people across the Jordan, to deliver us into the hands of the Amorites to destroy us? The Canaanites and the other people of the country will hear of our defeat and will surround us and wipe our name from the earth. What then will you do for your own great name, O mighty Elohim?' All these things I did ask of God on behalf of Israel."

Joshua was silent, looking down as he paced, his robe swirling with each sharp turn. The dust trailed him, as did the eyes of the army of Israel, waiting for his answers. Finally Joshua halted and looked up, rigid. "The Lord answered me," he thundered. " 'Stand up,' He said to me. 'What are you doing on your face? Israel has *sinned!*' " Joshua thrust both fists at the sky.

"The Lord told me that one among us has violated the command He gave us when we defeated Jericho. One among us has taken some of the devoted things, he has stolen, he has lied, he has put them with his own possessions. That is why we could not withstand our enemies." He shook his fists at the men. "That is why we turn our backs and run, because one among us has made us liable to destruction."

The thunder of Joshua's wrath ceased, and only silence vibrated the bright morning air. No one looked at his neighbor, but each looked inward, fearful, searching his memories for fear he had taken any object from the ruins of Jericho.

"Elohim has said, 'I will be with Israel no longer unless you destroy whatever among you is devoted to destruction. Go,' He told me, 'and consecrate the people in preparation, for this is what the Lord God of Israel says to the people. Destroy that which is devoted among you, O Israel. You cannot stand against your enemies until you remove it.' "

Joshua's arms fell limp at his side. "Spend this day in consecration. In the morning, present yourselves tribe by tribe. He who is caught with the devoted things shall be destroyed by fire, along with all that belongs to him."

The next morning dawned with an unusual stillness, as if even the breeze hid, fearing discovery. The silent men of Israel straggled into the red and dreadful dawn. Lining up with his tribesmen, Hanniel stretched his still-aching muscles and awaited the words of their leader, who conferred with Eleazer, the high priest.

Eleazer opened his hand to show Joshua the two unmarked stones he palmed. The morning's first sunlight glanced off the rocks, and Hanniel knew Eleazer would use the holy Urim and Thummim to discover Israel's traitor. He shivered. *Better never to have been born than to have the sacred rocks single you out today.*

Each tribe came forward, one by one, to be either exonerated or condemned by a toss of the holy Urim and Thummim stones. Simeon, Issachar, and Benjamim presented themselves before the high priest, and as each tribe was found innocent they circled back to watch the others' fate.

Manasseh was next in line. Hanniel stood with his tribesmen in solemn prayer that none of theirs had sinned. The holy stones that spoke God's will thudded in the dust.

Eleazer shook his head, and Joshua motioned the tribe away.

Next Judah stood before the high priest. The stones hit the ground. Eleazer looked up slowly at Joshua and nodded. Joshua rose. "The Lord has taken the tribe of Judah."

Not a sound, not a movement came from Judah, but the rest of camp heaved a collective sigh of relief. "Come forward now, clan by clan," Joshua commanded the men of Judah.

The sun climbed toward its zenith, adding the torrid heat of summer's end to the weight of anxiety. Eleazer began the laborious process of casting lots for the many clans of Judah. Hanniel watched each trembling clan advance like a many-membered body to stand before the high priest, and then fall away in a near faint when the finger of God passed them by.

The sun had scorched its way through the burden and heat of the day when the clan of Zerahite came forward. A weary Eleazer threw the stones again. The lot was cast.

"Lord God of the Universe!" Zerahite shouted into the dust as he fell with a cry, followed by each family in his clan. "Do not overcome us with Your wrath. We will offer up to You the one who sinned against You, only do not destroy us completely."

Family by family, the clan of Zerahite came forward and receded as the toss of the stones exempted them from guilt. The family of Zimri stood before Joshua. Again Eleazer tossed the Urim and Thummim. The family of Zimri was taken. Hanniel knew not how the silence of the day could deepen further, but the quiet grew until he dared not even breathe, as he watched each man in Zimri's family come before the high priest.

The one called Achan knelt trembling in the dirt. The stones were thrown. Hanniel heard them clack together. The Urim fell to its blank side. The Thummim rolled past it, slowing, pulling itself over again and again, as if weary from its day's work, tipped on its edge and balanced for an eternity between yes and no, then fell with a whack to yes.

"What have you done, man?" Joshua barked. Achan buried his face in the dirt and trembled. "My son, give glory to the Lord God of Israel. Turn back to Him and tell me the truth. Do not hide it from me!"

Achan sprang from his crouch. "It is true!" he cried. "I have sinned against the Lord. I saw in the plunder of Jericho a beautiful robe from Babylon and two hundred shekels of silver and a fifty-shekel wedge of gold. The gold was for me, but the Babylonian mantle was for my wife. She asked me to get one for her." He held out his upturned palms as he spoke, as if he would be excused. Then he lowered his arms and his head. In a low voice, heavy with resignation, he said, "They are hidden in the ground inside my tent."

Joshua dispatched two trusted captains to dig up the articles and then addressed Achan. "Why have you brought disaster upon us?"

The coils of grief and frustration tightened with anger inside Hanniel and sprang loose. He hurled himself through the throng of men to face Achan.

"You wanted them? How many men are dead because of your greed? How many orphans have you added to Israel this day? How many wives are widows now because of you?" Everything around Hanniel melted into blurs of sun-streaked colors, except for the whitened face of Achan. He bore down on him. "My cousin, Achan, my cousin is now a widow because of you! Was it worth it?"

Hanniel grabbed Achan's shoulders and shook him. "Was it worth it?" he bellowed, towering over him. Achan slung his head from side to side. Hanniel shook him harder. "Was it?"

"No," Achan whimpered.

And then Hanniel realized he contended not with Achan but with Elohim. Even if Achan had not caused Ludim's death, Hanniel would still be subject to Elohim and it seemed that His will was for him to lose Rizpah. He felt the press of hands on his shoulders and heard vague voices calling his name, and Caleb was at his side, soothing him, pulling him away.

"Achan!" Joshua thundered. "You have brought disaster on the entire nation because of your sin. Today the Lord will bring disaster on you."

Hanniel stared as the Levites dragged Achan away. The condemned man made no attempt to resist, and all the fight drained from Hanniel too. Every circumstance made Elohim's will clear. Hanniel would make no further attempt to resist it.

15

"So the lost sheep has been found."

Hanniel smiled to himself when he heard Caleb's slow drawl behind him. "I didn't know I was lost."

"Well, you were to me. I couldn't find you."

"If I'd known you were looking I'd have left a trail."

The two men smiled and then looked westward, out over the plain of Jericho where they camped at Gilgal. The sun sank behind the mountains abruptly. The quick change from heat to cool shadow made sunset Hanniel's favorite time. Israel's fast-falling night left no space for lingering, no agonized waiting; the sky was either light or dark, no dusky indecision.

"You could have left an ample trail with the food you left at supper." Caleb cleared his throat as he squinted at the horizon. "The women told me you haven't eaten all day." Hanniel shifted on the boulder where he sat. "Are you so disturbed by your cousin's death?" When Hanniel was silent Caleb continued. "Is it the stoning of Achan and his family today?" Silence. "A mixture of both?"

Hanniel looked out over the

darkened plain, feeling the usual shiver start at his neck from the drop in temperature.

"Ludim didn't have a chance," Hanniel began in a husky voice.

Caleb squatted next to him and listened to the story of Ludim's death. He uttered no sound except to breathe a grim, "You had only a pickax?"

Before Hanniel came to Ludim's dying wish he stopped, dwelling on the thoughts that had distracted him all day. Could he truly resign himself to giving up Rizpah? Was Ludim's request really binding? After all, Zelophehad had all but asked Caleb to marry Rizpah on his deathbed, and Caleb felt no obligation to his wishes. Still, Ludim's request could be Elohim's way of telling Hanniel he'd misinterpreted the signals. What if he *were* never meant to marry her? The thought was difficult to accept. He'd been so sure—once. *I must try once more to marry her, and if she refuses yet again I will know the will of Elohim for certain.* Surely he could win Rizpah now. He turned to confide his decision to his new friend when a young boy ran toward them in the early darkness.

"Joshua has called a meeting at the campfires," he shouted. "Hurry."

Caleb reached out and caught the boy's sleeve as he ran past them. "Wait, son. For what purpose is this meeting called? Do you know?"

The boy bobbed his head, his face flushed with the privilege of bearing this important news. "He will explain the battle plans for marching on Ai again."

Expectant rays of sunlight glanced off Hanniel's sword as he marched with Manasseh, Gad, and Reuben at the head of the army of Israel. The ground vibrated with the steady tread of avenging Israelites advancing on the unsuspecting city of Ai. The townspeople had probably spent the previous day in drunken celebration of their victory over these wandering shepherds who, as rumor had it, were the blessed property of a God who had parted two mighty waters for them to pass through. *Now,* Hanniel snorted to himself, *they will learn how powerful is the Lord God of Israel.*

A spark of sunlight reflected off the tower of the city gates, and Hanniel knew the king had been alerted. He imagined how cocky their army must feel as he watched the city gates open wide and Ai's army pour through them to meet the Israelites. His mouth curved into a knowing smile, but his eyes held the dull chill of unpolished iron. These were the people who had resisted Elohim's command to surrender the land to His people. These were the people who had ambushed Ludim. Today they would be taught to fear the one true God. Today they and their temples and false idols would fall.

The army of Ai raced confidently to meet the Israelites in the valley of Arabah, beneath the hill that housed their city. *For now,* Hanniel thought, *let them imagine they will trounce us as before.*

Hanniel scanned the northwest area behind and between Ai and Bethel, where thirty thousand Israelites lay in wait. To the west, another five thousand hid, close by Ai. If things went according to Joshua's divine plan of attack, the neighboring city of Bethel would also answer the battle cry until only a handful would be left to protect Ai.

As if his thoughts were the catalyst, as the front lines of Ai's army clashed with Israel down in the valley, the king of Bethel led his army in chase, whooping and sounding their trumpets.

Ai's front ranks penetrated as far as Manasseh before Joshua gave the secret signal to retreat. A gruff, red-skinned Canaanite raced toward Hanniel, brandishing his sword. As much as it galled Hanniel to play the coward, he ran as instructed, his feet keeping time to the mocking laughter of the enemy.

Israel fled to the hills of the Arabah desert. Hanniel

glanced back to see that the entire armed forces of both cities pursued them and the Arabah valley held only a few of the rear ranks. The "victors" scrambled after them up the rocky hills, the thirst for Israel's blood hastening their chase.

The pre-established blasts on the shofar sounded, so long and loud and piercing that Ai's army hesitated in confusion at the untimely victory trump. Hanniel looked up to the soaring desert hill where Joshua stood tall, holding out a javelin.

Squaring his shoulders, Hanniel pivoted to face the soldier at his heels. He took a purposeful step toward the man, his expression revealing his harrowing intent, and the soldier drew back. A cry arose from the Canaanite army, and every man in the blistering desert turned his eyes to see the first black clouds billow from the doomed city. The soldier in front of Hanniel turned back to him, understanding dimming his eyes as he fought for his life. Israel rushed upon the two armies. Ai and Bethel, realizing their plight, retreated, and were halted by the sight of thousands of Israelites pouring through their gates from within the burning city. They were surrounded.

Hanniel opened his eyes slowly, but everything was murky and dark. The cold stone of the Arabah dug at his back. The desert swirled around him. He blinked repeatedly to clear his vision. His last conscious thought was of fighting sword to sword, the smoke of the burning city blending with the lengthening afternoon shadows. *But we were winning,* Hanniel determined. *Why am I alone on my back amid the icy hills of the wilderness?*

A scuffle of feet snapped his mind to attention. Hanniel groped for his sword and spied it a few spans past his reach. He lifted his shoulder to retrieve the weapon and a pain that originated in his right thigh seared through his side, knocking him back into a near faint. In a split second he took in the spectral light of the rising moon splashed over dozens of still, foreign bodies all around him. *I must have been mistaken for a Canaanite and left for dead.*

Clutching his right thigh, he fought to remain alert. The scuffling came closer, but the swirling darkness in his brain was forming soft cushions beneath him. Though Hanniel took deep gulps of the cold night air, he felt himself floating away on the fleecy bed of inertia.

The reddish hue that penetrated his closed eyes told Hanniel it was morning, and the flat ground and woven texture of the blanket beneath him assured him he was back in camp. A shofar's muffled blare blew away the last mists of unconsciousness. Hanniel opened his eyes.

"...and I personally saw a dozen men fall by his sword, Commander." A young soldier stood with Joshua beside Hanniel.

"Yes. Others have also told me of this man's bravery in the face of battle."

Hanniel tried to address Joshua, but the words came out garbled. Israel's commander leaned over to hear. Hanniel jerked as if to snap to attention, but a pain shot through his right leg and burst in his side. Clutching his thigh, he fell back, dizzy.

"The emergency is over." Joshua put out his hand to Hanniel. "You have already contributed more than your due."

Hanniel blinked to clear his thoughts. Looking around him, he saw a number of women caring for about a half dozen injured men in a large tent. "Those men are wounded," he said woodenly, and then looked down at his right thigh bound tightly with clean white linen.

"Yes," Joshua laughed. "but only a handful were wounded, and *all* live!"

Hanniel concentrated on the cloth around his leg. "This material is fine linen. Where—"

"Let the finest Canaanite cloth bind the wounds of our nation." Joshua boomed.

"Wounds?" Hanniel finally realized his plight.

"But not serious," Joshua hurried to explain. "Yours was a clean cut. It should heal very quickly. Of course, you may have a slight limp, but..." His voice trailed off.

Hanniel looked at Joshua. "You came here to tell me this?"

Joshua shook his head. "I am told of the many Canaanites who fell by your sword yesterday, but that is not what brings me to your bedside either. I expect that kind of bravery from all my men. It is for your valor when Ai *defeated* us that I come to you. Your action to save your cousin in the quarry is commendable. That is the kind of courage I would wish I could expect for all my men."

"But there was no one else—"

Joshua beamed down at him.

"Caleb?" Hanniel asked, and Joshua nodded.

"I commend you." Joshua's face grew serious as he reached down to place his hands on Hanniel's head for a blessing.

Hanniel stared up at his commander in awe, humbled by the recognition. He opened his mouth to protest but Joshua interrupted with a knowing smile.

"Save your strength, man." The shofar blasted again and Joshua nodded. "You and the other wounded will be carried later to Mount Ebal, where I will give the Law. All of Israel gathers there now. On the mount we will build a great altar to the Lord." Joshua's eyes misted as he spoke, glinting with an inner fever, and Hanniel only nodded. He knew today would be one he would never forget.

"Sir?" Joshua returned his gaze to Hanniel. "My cousin who died...he left behind a widow—a widow who is also my cousin. I would like permission to travel back to Gilead. This news will be hard for her. I think it would go better for her if I am the one to tell her."

"Of course. You'll need time to let your leg heal and being among your family will hasten your recovery. Return with us when we march again next spring."

16

The clear, crisp blue of the cloudless sky dipped into the valleys surrounding Mount Ebal as if to push the mountain, teeming with workmen, into the heavens. To Hanniel, reclining outside the infirmary, the infinite arms of Elohim seemed to have reached down to cup this particular mountain. It stood against the sky, an etching in forest and mud and rock, visible to all for miles.

No wonder Elohim chose this place, Hanniel thought as he remembered the command of God through Moses.

> And when you have passed over the Jordan, you shall set up stones on Mount Ebal. There you shall build an altar to the Lord your God. And when He brings you into the land you are entering to occupy, there on Mount Gerizim you shall pronounce the blessing and on Mount Ebal the curse.

Mindless of his throbbing leg, Hanniel impatiently signalled one of the women tending the wounded. "Have someone carry me to the mountaintop now." When she started to argue, pointing at his leg, Hanniel waved her away. "Do it now," he snapped. Then, sorry for his outburst, he called her back. "I can't see what they are about from here," he explained apologetically.

The woman gave him a nervous smile and went to fetch the men. Watching her hasty retreat, Hanniel berated himself for the way he had treated her. If Rizpah were fussing over his injury, he would have been flattered. *It must be the continual dull pain in my leg,* Hanniel decided.

Four muscular men were needed to lift Hanniel to a stretcher made of rushes and reeds. Closing his eyes, he allowed the sun to melt away the tension in his body as he was borne up the slopes of Mount Ebal. As he succumbed to the sun's therapy, his mind strayed to a favorite vision—Rizpah, throwing open her arms to his proposal. Only this time would be different. She would fall on his chest when he returned to Gilead, and she would cry, "How could I have refused your love for so long?"

He searched into the future to appraise their sons and daughters, sturdy of body like himself, and strong of character like Rizpah. *Oh, but won't children like that give me trouble!* Hanniel chuckled to himself. But in the corner of his dream, the figure of the widowed Hoglah crouched, forever sobbing her loneliness.

"The shade of the oaks will make a comfortable booth for you," said one of the men as they lowered Hanniel's bed onto the cool grass atop Mount Ebal. They left him quickly, to help the rest of the army carry stones up the mountain to build the altar. Already Hanniel could see the circle of stones rising, as each man deposited his field stones at Joshua's feet. Caleb stood beside the commander, overseeing construction.

Taking a deep breath of the cool, mountain air, Hanniel looked around him. From this peak he spotted the snows of Mount Hermon in the north, looking like a heavenly field of cotton. The rippling azure waters of the Great Sea sparkled in the west. Twisting to see the southern view behind him, he glimpsed the hills round about Jerusalem, the unconquerable Jebusite city. The mountains of Gilead were visible across the Jordan to the east, where Rizpah awaited him.

Peering down into the valley between Mount Ebal and Gerizim, Hanniel appraised the gates of Shechem, closed tight at midmorning. He chuckled. Apparently the city had heard about the plundering Israelites and had chosen to avoid confrontation.

As the altar rose to its full height, Hanniel noticed some men hauling large jugs and chalices to its base. The construction must be nearly complete. Caleb stretched and looked around, spotting Hanniel beneath the grove of oaks, and he crossed the distance with long strides.

"I didn't know that you came up," he said as he squatted beside him. Then pointing to the altar, "It will completed in a few moments. Joshua will begin the reading of the law soon."

"Joshua visited me this morning."

"Oh, that," Caleb said casually. "I *told* him *anyone* would have done the same under the same circumstances."

They laughed, and Hanniel clapped his hand upon Caleb's shoulder. "You are my friend."

Caleb nodded.

"Joshua gave me permission to go home to Gilead."

"He told me."

"I must be the one to tell Hoglah." Hanniel stared off at the distant mountains of Lebanon and wondered again if he should confide Ludim's request to Caleb.

"I think that is wise. She will need your strength."

"So I've been told," Hanniel said under his breath.

"What?"

"Nothing."

The shofar sounded. "It is time for Israel to gather. I must go now. You will be able to see well from here."

Hanniel gripped Caleb's hand as he rose. "I leave in the morning. I may not see you before I go."

"There is no need for good-byes among brothers."

Briskly Caleb released Hanniel's hand and hurried to Joshua's side.

The priests lit the wood on top of the altar, and then Eleazer, the high priest, stepped forward. A young bullock and a ram and a goat, all male and without blemish, were led braying to the smoldering altar. After laying his hands upon the head of each beast in solemn consecration, Eleazer unsheathed a long, narrow-blade dagger. One by one he leaned his hand again upon the animals' heads, this time guiding them to the north side of the altar for slaughter. He caught the flowing blood in one of the vessels Hanniel had seen carted up the mountain. First sprinkling some of it on the side of the stones, he emptied what remained at the base of the altar.

Kneeling beside each animal the priest flayed them, tossing the skins into a pile to be burned outside camp, and cut the sacrifices into small pieces. He washed the intestines and hind legs, including the head and the fat, and then laid those parts upon the crackling wood to be consumed.

Eleazer raised his hands to the sky. "O mighty and gracious Lord God, the congregation of Your people, Israel, renew our complete surrender to live a consecrated life, pleasing to You. Please accept our offering. May it be a pleasing scent to You." He stood with his back to Israel until the remains of the offering had gone up in smoke, two of his sons supporting his uplifted arms for him at the last.

New wood was lighted on the altar and ten male and ten female oxen were led in for the peace offering. Eleazer slaughtered the animals and poured out their blood the same as before, then cut out the animals' fat and intestines, and burned them separately. He separated the breast and the right shoulder of each, the shoulder being laid aside as the portion for the high priest and Levites. The breasts of the oxen were waved before the altar, symbolically presented to the Lord, and the priests then accepted them for their own use. These two portions of each animal were taken by

Eleazer's sons and roasted upon a spit to the left and the remaining flesh of the twenty beasts was cooked on spits to the right, for the people of the congregation. The nation stood in reverent prayer as Eleazer gave the benediction and the meat cooked.

Again the high priest lifted his arms to heaven. "We offer to You, O Lord, this sacrifice of peace because of the peace we have found under Your divine grace. We thank You for accepting our offering and establishing us as Your people, a holy nation under You."

The aroma of roasted meat wafted over the nation as they stood, half covering the slopes of Mount Ebal, half on the side of Mount Gerizim. Levites carried the cooked meat from the spits on the right of the altar among the people, and they each took one bite to finalize the offering while the high priest ate his portion alone.

As Hanniel chewed the savory meat he, along with all the people, vowed a life of commitment to Elohim Hayyim and to His laws. So at peace with God was Hanniel that he felt assured Rizpah would accept his final proposal; but he vowed to God an unbreakable oath that if Rizpah turned him down, he would ask Hoglah to marry him. The decision settled, he turned his thoughts to worship.

Joshua stood and recited all the law of God. All of Israel stood assembled, slaves as well as Israelites, the women and the children, with their elders and officers and their judges. The people stood on opposite sides of the mountain and watched the priests carry the ark of the covenant of the Lord up the slopes so it could be seen by all as the concrete symbol of God's covenant with them.

When Joshua finished, the Levites gathered around the altar and recited to the people in a loud voice.

"Cursed is the man who carves an image or casts an idol—a thing detestable to the Lord, the work of the craftsman's hands—and sets it up in secret."

And all the people shouted, "Amen!"

"Cursed is the man who dishonors his father or his mother."

And all the people shouted, "Amen!"

"Cursed is the man who moves his neighbor's boundary stone."

And all the people shouted, "Amen!"

"Cursed is the man who leads the blind astray on the road."

And all the people shouted, "Amen!"

"Cursed is the man who withholds justice from the alien, the fatherless, or the widow."

And all the people shouted, "Amen!"

"Cursed is the man who sleeps with his father's wife, for he dishonors his father's bed."

And all the people shouted, "Amen!"

"Cursed is the man who has sexual relations with any animal."

And all the people shouted, "Amen!"

"Cursed is the man who sleeps with his sister, the daughter of his father or the daughter of his mother."

And all the people shouted, "Amen!"

"Cursed is the man who sleeps with his mother-in-law."

And all the people shouted, "Amen!"

"Cursed is the man who kills his neighbor secretly."

And all the people shouted, "Amen!"

"Cursed is the man who accepts a bribe to kill an innocent person."

And all the people shouted, "Amen!"

"Cursed is the man who does not uphold the words of this law by carrying them out."

And all the people shouted, "Amen!"

The mountains echoed with the voices of a nation, penetrating Hanniel's heart to the depths in the chill of the sunset. The day had waned with the lengthy rituals, but no one minded, least of all Hanniel. The words touched off an ember that glowed in every Israelite, fanning into that unifying flame that held them together as a nation, that caused them to look on one another as brothers.

Its flame was their purpose in persevering, it was their very indentity, it was what made them a chosen people; chosen to bring the light of Elohim to a dark and dreadful world. Today the nation sensed a dramatic revelation of all that they had experienced and all that was to come, and no one wanted it to end.

In the dusk the tribes of Reuben, Gad, Asher, Zebulun, Dan and Naphtali, who stood on the side of Mount Ebal, began to recite the curses God had warned would come upon them if they failed to obey His laws.

"If you do not obey the Lord your God, all these curses will come upon you and overtake you. You will be cursed in the city and cursed in the country. Your basket and your kneading trough will be cursed. The fruit of your womb will be cursed, and the crops of your land, and the calves of your herds and the lambs of your flocks. You will be cursed when you come in and cursed when you go out. The Lord will turn the rain of your country into dust and powder. The Lord will cause you to be defeated before your enemies. You will come at them from one direction but flee from them in seven. All these curses will come upon you. They will pursue you and overtake you until you are destroyed, because you did not obey the Lord and observe the commands and decrees He gave you."

When the final echoes of the curses bounced off the mountainsides around them and disappeared, the tribes of Simeon, Levi, Judah, Issachar, Joseph, and Benjamin raised their arms to recite the blessings from the side of Mount Gerizim. Their voices united with an urgency to obtain them.

"You will be blessed in the city and blessed in the country. The fruit of your womb will be blessed, and the crops of your land and the young of your livestock—the calves of your herds and the lambs of your flocks. Your basket and your kneading trough will be blessed. You will be blessed when you come in, and blessed when you go out. The Lord will grant that the enemies who rise up against you will be defeated before you. They will come at you from one direction but flee from you in seven.

"The Lord will send a blessing on your barns and on everything you put your hand to. The Lord your God will bless you in the land He is giving you. The Lord will establish you as His holy people, as He promised you on oath, if you keep the commands of the Lord your God and walk in His ways. Then all the peoples on earth will see that you are called by the name of the Lord, and they will fear you. The Lord will grant you abundant prosperity—in the fruit of your womb, the young of your livestock, and the crops of your ground—in the land He swore to your forefathers to give you. The Lord will open the heavens, the storehouse of His bounty, to send rain on your land in season and to bless all the work of your hands. You will lend to many nations but will borrow from none. The Lord will make you the head, not the tail. Do not turn aside from any of the commands I give you today, to the right or to the left, following other gods and serving them."

Every star in the heavens sparkled, brilliant with the promise of the future.

די

Rizpah followed her brother-in-law, Reuben, into his tent and stopped. The warmth and vitality of the newlyweds' home assaulted her. The impact on Rizpah was not pleasant; it only emphasized her loneliness. Reuben tapped her shoulder and pointed at Tirzah. His wife lay on a bed mat criss-crossed with layers of rushes from the banks of the river Yarmuk. Tirzah moaned. Rizpah knelt to place a thin, chapped hand on her sister's pregnant belly.

"Where is the pain the strongest?"

"It hurts worst low in my back."

Rizpah nodded. "Does your stomach cramp at all?"

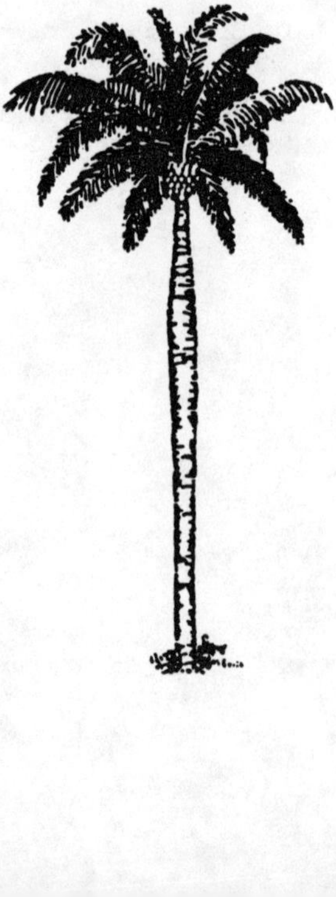

"Yes—" Tirzah caught her breath as another pain rolled through her.

"Show me where."

Tirzah took Rizpah's hand and drew it to the underside of her stomach mound. Rizpah felt a wave press through. "I didn't think your time was yet."

"It is not." Reuben's voice quivered as he knelt beside her.

Rizpah saw the panic that lined his eyes. "When did you expect—"

"Not for a month. What is wrong?"

"It may be nothing. Women often have pains before they actually deliver."

Tirzah gave a soft moan, and Reuben jumped. "But her pain is so great!"

"Birthing is hard work."

"I thought you said she wasn't—"

"There is more to birthing than the delivery." Rizpah's tone was matter-of-fact.

"But isn't it hard on the baby to be born before his time?"

"If you will do everything I say, the baby may stay where it is awhile longer."

"I don't want to know about the 'ifs,' " Reuben sprang from his kneeling position. "I want to know how to stop this."

"If you panic, you can be of no help to your wife."

"Don't treat me like a child." He grabbed Rizpah's arms. "My baby will die if he is delivered this soon, won't he? And what of Tirzah? If the baby dies, will she—"

His wife reached out and touched his leg. "Reuben, don't—" A pain caught her words away, and she clutched at the sheets.

Rizpah slung Reuben's hands off. "Listen to me. I don't think the baby will die. I won't lie to you: she is too early; but I feel we can bring Tirzah *and* the baby through this."

"You don't *think* the baby will die? You *feel* we can bring them through? You say that so calmly. You've hardly seen Tirzah since we moved to Gilead. You never came when she could have used your help because you were grieving over Caleb, and now you act as if you don't care that she may—" Reuben stopped at the look on Rizpah's face.

Have mercy on me, Lord, God! Rizpah cried. *Is this what I've done to my family?* With quick estimation she realized summer was over and they'd lived in Gilead over five months now. Where had the time gone? Had she truly been so lost in her grief? The restless nights, shredded with dreams haunted by Caleb and the forty phantom years of her wasted life, and the listless days, secluded in her secret place in the cliffs...Reuben's words forced the truth before her, and she almost staggered under their burden.

Reuben coughed. "Forgive me. You are to blame for none of this." He stared down at his wife. "She just looks so ...sick."

Rizpah set her guilt aside to deal with later. "She is not sick, she's pregnant, and she needs our help."

"I know," Reuben said in a low voice.

"Good. Now, what was she doing when the pains started?"

"Ummm...the washing, I think."

"The washing? Down by the river? What were you thinking of, letting her climb into that gorge when she is so big with child?"

Reuben looked as if he'd been whipped. "I didn't know...I never thought..." Then his voice was defensive. "I wasn't even here. I didn't know what she had planned."

Rizpah laid her hand on his cheek and patted. "I'm sorry. This is no more your fault than mine."

"I've been working in the fields," he murmured. "Bringing in the last harvest has kept me away most of the time. She has been wrestling in her sleep the last few nights. I didn't know it could be because of *this*." Tirzah moaned again.

"Go boil some water and dip linen in it. Then split open a leather pouch. Wrap the hot linen in the skin and bring it to me."

Reuben hurried to obey, and Rizpah knelt beside Tirzah. She wadded a blanket and pushed it under the small of Tirzah's back. With both hands she traced continuous feathery circles around her sister's protruding belly. "This will help you relax." Rizpah continued until Tirzah moaned again, then helped her to the mat. She removed the wadded blanket and massaged the aching back.

"Here." Reuben handed her the steaming leather bag he'd prepared.

Rizpah wrapped it in a blanket and placed the bag on Tirzah's stomach, pulling her covers tight around her. "Do you see how I massage her back?" Reuben nodded. "You do the same while I go tell the family what has happened."

She returned with Milcah, Hoglah, and her three daughters, and the promise that Mahlah would be carried over as soon as possible. Reuben hardly noticed their entrance, dabbing at Tirzah's temples with a cool, wet strip of linen.

"Oh, Tirzah, dear," Milcah trilled in an unnatural voice, sweeping across the room. "If you'd have let me know you were in pain I would have done your work for you. This needn't have happened." She sat to one side of Tirzah, patting her hand.

Rizpah watched, Milcah's false laughter ringing in her ears. Her sister was different. With a jolt she realized Milcah had not been spending from dawn to dark with the flocks out of necessity; she had been working out her own grief over losing Othniel. Rizpah had been burrowed so deep within her self-pity she had not noticed Milcah's state. Now she understood why Milcah's bubbly gaiety and almost flirtatious manner had so annoyed her; it was forced. Rizpah's heart, now that she'd made room in it for another sorrow other than her own, ached for her sister.

The front tent flap whipped aside and Mahlah was carried in by her new husband, Nathan, and fifteen-year-old stepson, Hemath. The invalid surveyed the scene. She whispered to Nathan, who then placed her chair at the head of Tirzah's bed.

"How are you, my darling?" Mahlah smoothed Tirzah's damp hair. Tirzah crinkled her eyes in a weak imitation of her impish smile, then sighed and closed her eyes.

"Reuben, you're a good husband," Mahlah said. "I think she's relaxed enough to sleep. Though I don't see how," she turned to Milcah with a smile, "with you pounding on her hand like that."

Milcah's lips stretched across her skeletal cheeks in a grin, revealing an alarming loss of weight. "I didn't even realize I was doing it."

Rizpah instinctively probed her own midriff and was surprised to feel her protruding ribs. She withdrew her hands in shock and stared at the thin, knobby extremities. What had she and Milcah been doing to themselves?

"I know you're scared, dear." Mahlah's words seemed to intimate a deeper meaning that did not penetrate Milcah's glazed grin. "So am I. You might feel less anxious, though, if you busied yourself while she rests. Maybe you could help Hoglah prepare supper." Mahlah leaned over and kissed Milcah's head, then turned to Reuben. "Would you bring me a bowl of cool water and a cloth to wash her face?"

As Tirzah's two attendants hurried to do Mahlah's bidding, Rizpah retrieved the cooled leather pouch and smiled at Mahlah. Mahlah returned a tentative, questioning smile. *She knows,* thought Rizpah, and was comforted.

Rizpah dipped the linen in boiling water and wrapped it again in the pouch, thinking how the scene so artfully illustrated the place each of her family possessed, taking notice of them with a fondness like one who has returned from a long journey.

Tirzah, even in her condition, was the joy of them all, drawing the family together. Milcah graced the scene with her perfect beauty, even though it was marred by her macabre efforts to disguise the heartache of losing Othniel. Hoglah, ever the sensible one, saw to the physical needs of everyone, and Mahlah, the regal mother figure of the family, brought organization, comfort, and love to the situation.

And what is my place? Rizpah wondered if, by her grieving separation from them, she was in danger of losing it. For the second time she felt her inheritance as a family member threatened. As with her father's blessing, she knew if it was, it was by her own hand. Replacing the warm bag under Tirzah's blankets, she joined Milcah and Hoglah in preparing supper, resuming her rightful place among them.

The meal was eaten in quiet around a huge pot of lentils. Rizpah enjoyed the silent companionship. Since Mahlah had married Nathan, there was only Milcah left to share the huge family tent with her, and the two had scarcely been good company for each other.

With renewed appreciation she studied the faces surrounding her. She watched Mahlah cast a girlish glance at her new husband. *Nathan,* thought Rizpah, *is probably the only man in all Israel with the character to see that Mahlah, though lame, is the perfect wife.* Nathan's unmarried son, Hemath, refilled Mahlah's bowl and handed it to her with a wink. Rizpah could see that Mahlah's love had revitalized the two lonely men.

The typically thoughtful Hoglah had taken a portion of the food and herded her three noisy daughters home to eat, so they wouldn't awaken Tirzah. Her absence was felt, but her presence in preparing the fare had reestablished an aura of well-being about the tent. Reuben ate hardly at all, periodically checking on his wife. He was exactly the kind of husband Tirzah deserved: not only a good provider, but a bountiful provider; not only caring, but protective; not only loving, but doting. Milcah sat next to Reuben, mincing mouthfuls of barley bread. How heartbreaking to discover the way she was grieving over Othniel. Though Milcah laughed more than ever, her eyes were blank and dull.

Excited shouts from neighbors disrupted Rizpah's musings. The family, as one, glared at the doorway as if in reprimand.

Milcah ran to the door. "What is it?" she asked an old woman who was running past.

"A detachment of our soldiers has arrived."

Milcah twirled toward them, her eyes sparkling, and Rizpah knew she hoped for Othniel to be among the soldiers.

Before anyone could speak, she was gone.

"Reuben, you go with Nathan and Hemath to meet them. I'll stay with Tirzah," Mahlah offered. She looked long at Rizpah, and Rizpah wondered if the hope of seeing Caleb again was as evident in her eyes as the longing was in Milcah's.

"Why don't you go too?" Mahlah said.

Rizpah left with deliberate casualness.

18

A train of over one hundred donkeys and camels was being penned outside the village, the animals snorting, braying, and staggering under the weight of their burdens. Townspeople milled about them and shouted to their families, holding up the treasures of the caravan. Rizpah saw gold chalices, fine twisted linen, silver, jewelry, precious stones, elegant purple, silks, incense, spices, perfumes, painted pottery, woven baskets, embroidered blankets and scarves, delicate sandals, and every sort of extravagance she could imagine. There were also grains, dried fruits and fish, leather, ropes, grinding wheels, lumber, iron plows, and innumerable items of everyday existence, but no Caleb. Obviously the soldiers were all of Manasseh.

"What is all this?" Rizpah asked a soldier who was unpacking the donkeys.

He turned, and with a familiar, lopsided grin, thrust a small, heavy jar into her hands. "It's yours, that's what it is."

"Hanniel!"

"Rizpah," he greeted, grinning broadly.

Rizpah threw her arms around him, nearly whacking his head

with the jar in her hand, then quickly regained her composure. "Forgive me," she murmured. "I'm acting like a brazen woman. It is just so good to see you again."

"And you," he beamed, his coffee-colored eyes shining almost too brightly. "Well, look at it." He indicated the container.

Rizaph looked. In her hands she held a surprisingly heavy bottle, the deep blue of the Great Sea. She ran her fingers over the smooth, gleaming surface, feeling its marble-like coolness. Turning it over, she found a detailed etching of lilies, bulrushes, and peacocks that would have been lost in the bottle's deep-water opaqueness if it had not been traced with strokes of bright paint.

"It's beautiful," she breathed.

"It's of alabaster. Here." Hanniel pulled out the lid and pushed the jar to her nose.

Rizpah sniffed. The most tantalizing fragrance wafted into her nostrils, and she inhaled deeper. "It's nard!"

Hanniel's head bobbed. "Yes, and I've saved it especially for you."

"I thank you—truly." Her gaze caught his, then skittered away. "But what *is* all this?"

"I told you." Hanniel laughed. "Yours—or rather, all of yours." His arm swept toward the camp. "Wait a moment." He turned to instruct the soldiers in dividing the treasure, and after greeting Reuben and Nathan, showed them what portion was to go to Rizpah and the others.

"Now." He took Rizpah's arm and led her through the scrambling, shouting throng of people. "Now we can talk. I will tell you all about it."

Rizpah stopped. "You're limping."

"Come. Let's sit where it's quiet. I will tell you all."

Rizpah followed, laughing for the first time in months, as he pretended to hobble like an old sage, using a staff as a crutch. She couldn't remember ever seeing him so merry, but then, she had no way of knowing what manner of man he was. She had always known he favored her and so had always avoided him. At Tirzah's wedding everyone but she knew how accomplished he was on the lyre. Rizpah had not allowed Hanniel into her life at all until the night he saved her from Salu.

She feared liking him if she got to know him, for somehow that would cheapen her love for Caleb. Rizpah raised her eyebrows at the strange thoughts that invaded her mind this evening. Reuben's accusation seemed to have brought her grief into a healing light and she could see with a clarity she'd not known before. Somewhat surprised, but content, she looked sideways at Hanniel.

"This is the first time I've seen the place that will be my home." Hanniel made conversation as they approached the edge of the village. "Do you know it is already named by our great Manassite warrior, Jair?"

"No, I didn't," Rizpah answered. "But your dispute with the name is evident in your tone. Or is it a dispute with the man?"

Hanniel just smiled. "He speaks of this place as 'the tent village of Jair.' He boasts that after Canaan is subdued, he will return to conquer the Geshurites and Maacathites and establish cities that his numerous sons will rule. He will not be limited to one village in his honor, he speaks of all Bashan and northern Gilead as his. Now it is common to hear my men speak of home as Havvoth-Jair. I can't tell if they jest or not. But I fear, with Jair's determination and high self-esteem, we may have to get used to calling our dwelling after him."

Rizpah smiled, noticing that Hanniel's conversation was free of stuttering. *He must be comfortable with me now.* She was more comfortable, too, knowing that his notion of marrying her no longer stood between them.

They trudged beyond the village, entering the forest's river path. Rizpah inhaled the crisp, fresh air beneath the towering pine and terebinth and oak trees, and wondered that she hadn't noticed the beauty before. Her appreciation for this fertile homeland ripened in the cool, dusky evening. "Havvoth-Jair," she whispered, then said aloud, "I like the sound of it."

The spongy forest floor crackled beneath their steps. Rizpah thought how pleasant their tent village was, erected practically within the forest itself. How disheartening to move into the cramped, dirty cities when their men returned from the campaigns in Canaan. She knew the rebuilt city walls would offer more protection, but the sacrifice seemed too great.

"Let's sit here," Hanniel suggested.

Rizpah perched on a stump in a small clearing just inside the woods where dusk darkened. From their spot they could see the townspeople scurrying back and forth with their treasures, yet they were enclosed on three sides by lush mountain foliage. Rizpah noticed that Hanniel did not sit but leaned stiff-legged against a tree, keeping his weight on his good leg. She wanted to ask him again about his injury but decided to let him tell her in his own time.

He looked around, still grasping the staff. "This is a beautiful area. I'm glad I chose to settle in Gilead when the wars are through."

"This spot does not compare with my secret place." Rizpah pointed lamely north, toward the river Yarmuk, wondering why she had told him that.

"Are you alone often?"

Rizpah thought his question odd. She studied him for a moment in the last of the twilight. Hanniel's left eye crossed slightly in a look Rizpah recognized from the day he had proposed to her. Fearing that the scene might be repeated, she avoided his eyes.

"You never did tell me where all this came from." She held up her gift.

"It's booty from Ai. Other detachments were sent to the tribes of Gad and Reuben with their share." Hanniel paused. "Rizpah?"

Rizpah took a deep breath. From the tone of his voice she knew he was approaching the subject she feared, and she wasn't ready.

"Rizpah, you don't know how I've longed to see you all these months. It seems that nothing was settled when you left camp at Abel Shittim."

"What do you mean?"

"The...the kiss."

Rizpah jerked her head to stare at him. "The kiss?" He had caught her completely by surprise. "You didn't take heart in that?" The look on his face told plainly just how much he had hoped in it, and Rizpah regretted her bluntness. She went on gently. "It was just an emotional reaction."

"An emotional reaction?"

She nodded. "Because of all that had happened to me. I had just *proposed* to Caleb again and been turned down, like some brazen woman." Hanniel stared at her. "You walked into the midst of my being attacked! Hanniel, you saved me! How did you expect me to thank you?"

"The kiss was only a thank you?"

Rizpah knew it was more than that. Her father's death, her ordeal with Caleb, Malah's being attacked, her uncle's assault—all these things had overwhelmed her soul. When Hanniel had rescued her from Salu, a dam burst forth, and Hanniel had been the unfortunate recipient of the flood. The kiss was more than a thank you, but it was not what Hanniel thought it to be. Never mind that at the time she had suffered guilt because his kiss had aroused her. Never mind that she felt she had betrayed Caleb by responding. She had dismissed these things as the emotion of the moment, and she was surprised that Hanniel hadn't done the same.

His pale face circled shining eyes that reflected moonlight the way only tears can. Rizpah clenched her fists in irritation at his persistence and at her own foolishness. Life seemed to revel in hurting them, destroying their conflicting dreams. She thought of her love-hate emotions toward Caleb and regretted that now she played the same role to Hanniel. Why couldn't he forget her and find some sweet, young maiden who would cherish him and return the love he gave so freely?

"Forgive my bluntness," she murmured. "It's just that I'm surprised. I thought you knew that the kiss meant nothing."

"Nothing." The word was not a question, not a statement, but an echo of Rizpah's verdict. Hanniel slumped against the tree and avoided her eyes. "I have grave news."

Rizpah snapped upright. During war "grave news" could mean only one thing. "Caleb?" she breathed before she could stop herself.

Hanniel shook his head, irritated, "Ludim."

"I must go to Hoglah."

"She doesn't know yet. I came here to tell her."

"I will take you to her."

19

Hoglah sat cross-legged on the embroidered mat Mahlah had given her and stared through the thick silence of her tent.

Rizpah had not expected this reaction. She had been prepared to hold her sister's hysterical body through the night as she waded through her grief, but she didn't know how to respond to this silence. Next to her, where they both had stood to break the news, Hanniel swayed. She reached to steady him. Of course Ludim was Hanniel's cousin, too, and his death and Hanniel's long trip with an injury had drained him.

Hanniel removed Rizpah's arm. "G-go bring your family. She w-will need them."

Locating everyone was difficult in the celebrations. Mahlah and Reuben stayed with Tirzah, but Milcah, Nathan, and Hemath returned with Rizpah. They found Hoglah's three daughters whimpering alone in the far corner of the tent. Hanniel knelt beside Hoglah, despite the obvious pain to his injury, holding her limp hand as she stared.

Everyone rushed to comfort the widowed woman but pulled back in confusion when Hoglah refused to acknowledge them.

She only stared. Nathan and Hemath took Hanniel to a corner of the tent and made whispered inquiries of the death, while Milcah and Rizpah comforted the children.

Rizpah glanced at the men and was surprised to see how white Hanniel's face had grown, and that his eyes still shone bright, too bright. She supposed that men, though they were accustomed to the losses of battle, did not know how to handle dealing with widows.

"Son, are you ill?" Nathan asked.

"No, I'm fine. I am only worried about Hoglah."

At Hanniel's words they all looked at the pathetic figure sitting alone and still.

"Father!" Hemath's shrill cry cracked the silence. The two grabbed for Hanniel as he pitched to the floor. Hoglah blinked. A babble of voices exploded as Rizpah and Milcah rushed to help and the children cried out. Nathan and Hemath carried Hanniel to the bed mat and lowered him onto it.

"Really, I'm f-fine," Hanniel murmured. "There's no n-need for this. I'm just tired."

Rizpah clasped his face with both hands. "He is fevered."

"It's w-warm in here." He pulled her hands from his face.

Rizpah raised his robe to examine the injury, but Hanniel jerked the material back in place. "Hanniel, I must look at your leg. It may be the source of your illness."

"No. Do not uncover me," he mumbled, his eyes closing. "You must not. I cannot...the kiss...remember the..." His voice faded into unconsciousness, and Rizpah lifted his robe.

She gasped. "It is infected." Nathan and Hemath murmured agreement as they studied the swollen, black wound. They shook their heads solemnly, each aware of the slim chances of recovery.

"I remember a potion for this." They turned to look at Milcah. "When I took the sheep to higher ground with Father, one of the men with us was cut and took ill from it. I helped Father prepare a potion. I think I can remember it." She paused, thinking. "Hemath, I'll need you to gather herbs. Nathan, build me a fire outside the tent. Rizpah, get me Hoglah's grinding wheel. I'll need—" Milcah stopped and stared.

Hoglah had risen from the mat and, trance-like, made her way to Hanniel. The group around him parted. Staring down at his unconscious form, Hoglah knelt and drew the hem of her scarf across his face, wiping away the beads of sweat beginning to form on his fevered brow.

Mahlah threw a glance at the sleeping form of Tirzah and yawned, arranging her robe over her lifeless legs. She picked up her embroidery and resumed work on the hem of the baby tunic she was making. A rustle outside the door of Reuben's tent caught her attention. She stared into the darkness.

Rizpah stepped from the night shadows into the tent. Mahlah gasped. "Oh, it's you. You shouldn't pounce so on old women at such hours." Rizpah didn't smile. "What are you doing out so late?" Mahlah peered at her.

"I couldn't sleep."

Mahlah nodded and resumed her needlework. "Neither could I. How is Hoglah?"

"She fell asleep caring for Hanniel. She was like one who returned from death. I'm almost grateful Hanniel took sick, for her sake." Mahlah looked shocked. "I said, *almost*. No, Hanniel's condition is grave."

Mahlah shook her head. "Well, he is receiving the best of care. Hoglah would work into a fever herself to help anyone. I suppose it's that very nature that pulled her from her grief."

Rizpah nodded. The cool of the night tickled her spine and she drew her legs into the circle of her arms. The fire crackled beside Mahlah and glanced off her silver bracelet as it jerked with each stitch. Wolves bayed in the forest hills behind them, but the thin walls of the tent curtained them in with the protective blaze.

Rizpah cleared her throat, staring down at her knees. "I have treated my family shamefully."

Mahlah said nothing but watched her.

"In grieving over Caleb I shut you all out of my life. I suppose I thought that by shutting out everything I would shut out the pain also." Rizpah looked up. "Can you forgive me?"

"I could forgive you anything." Mahlah smiled. "I've been very concerned about you."

Rizpah peered at her sister, the sister she had always looked to for wisdom and counsel. "Why is life so complicated?"

"Sometimes I think we complicate it with our own interference." Mahlah looked into Rizpah's eyes. She whispered, "Are you all right now?"

Rizpah thought before she answered. "Not yet."

Mahlah squeezed Rizpah's hand, and no more words were needed.

Rizpah sighed and played with the frayed strap of her sandal, her chin resting on her knees. "I wish I could talk to Father right now."

"And I. I still grieve a little for him."

"Remember how, when we were young, he would grip our faces and shake them if we were sad?"

Mahlah smiled. "He said it was to scare the gloom bird from our heads."

"And then he would pretend he was chasing the bird around the room." Rizpah laughed. "Waving his arms and shouting wildly at it until he shooed it out the door." Rizpah's smile faded and she stared past Mahlah.

"Don't you ever wish it were yesterday?"

Rizpah trudged from Tirzah's tent and leaned for a moment against the door poles, thankful for their sturdy support and the shade from the afternoon sun supplied by the door flap stretched overhead. Shaking the dust from her headscarf, she wiped her dripping face. She had never been so overworked as in these past three days caring for Tirzah and helping Milcah with Hoglah's two youngest girls, not to mention worrying about the still-unconscious Hanniel. Hoglah had insisted he not be moved from her tent, so her children had to be watched. Rizpah was thankful they lived in the ever-lush mountains, so that Milcah no longer needed to travel for days to find grazing for their flocks. Still, she was gone most of each day, and only Hoglah's firstborn was old enough to accompany her, leaving the two youngest in Rizpah's charge until afternoon, when Mahlah relieved her.

The Lord in His wisdom has chosen younger women for such tasks, Rizpah thought, and she was reminded of Caleb, renowned for his wisdom. *Oh, yes, he had everything wrapped up neatly in the fine linen of his mind.* Remembering the wisdom he had used in rejecting her, she covered her face and pressed her sweaty eyelids tightly to force out the vision. *I must stop thinking of him! I will stop!* She knew she must, for the sake of her sanity and her family.

Gathering her skirt, Rizpah headed for Hoglah's tent. Each afternoon while Tirzah slept through the burden and heat of the day, she went to check on their cousin. Though winter was only a month away, and the heat was not so stifling now, all of Israel continued the traditional early afternoon rest. *Everyone sleeps except for me, that is.*

Hoglah lifted a flushed face to her greeting. "Ah, Rizpah!" She spoke in her low, sensible voice as she threw a bowl of murky water out the door. "I see you are not taking your rest again."

"If you were sleeping yourself, how would you know I am not?"

"Rizpah—always ready with an answer."

"Nevertheless, after caring so long for a fevered man, and with your—that is, under the circumstances, I would think you need rest more than I." Rizpah couldn't help noticing she didn't *look* like she needed rest.

"Our fevered patient is no longer—"

"What!" Rizpah bolted for the tent door, thinking that Hanniel had died.

Hoglah laughed. *The bereaved widow, laughing?* "Let me finish." She took Rizpah's arm. "Hanniel is no longer *fevered*. Come in and see, but be quiet; he is still very weak."

Rizpah blinked in the darkness of the tent, but she could make out the still figure of Hanniel. His delirious tossing was gone now, and he breathed the deep sleep of the recovered. Hoglah motioned Rizpah back outside.

"Let's sit under the doorway so we don't wake him."

Rizpah was thankful to be off her feet and settled down with a sigh. "Thanks be to Elohim for his restored life," she whispered.

Hoglah lifted thankful eyes heavenward, also, and then

picked up a reed platter to sift some freshly ground grain. "How is Tirzah today?"

"The same. Her labor has subsided, but if she moves at all it begins again. And Hanniel?" As usual Rizpah found conversation with Hoglah awkward. "When did his fever break?"

"About an hour ago." Hoglah shook the sifting plate as she spoke. "I have been so worried about him. I could do nothing but bathe his forehead and force down the teas Milcah prepared for him. She would not let me dress his festered wound, but she kept it clean and applied many oils she prepared from herbs and barks."

"I'm sorry I could be of no help."

"Oh, no, Rizpah, don't be. You were busy with Tirzah. I would never have called you from our sister. *I* am sorry I could not assist *you*."

A rustle inside the tent caught their attention and Hoglah leapt to Hanniel's side. Rizpah followed. Hoglah knelt beside the bed mat and murmured something to him. Rizpah stepped closer, hoping to speak with him.

"You have a visitor," Hoglah said softly.

Hanniel raised a shaky arm, and Rizpah stepped toward the mat. He clasped Hoglah's hand. Rizpah stopped. With tenderness in his raspy voice he spoke, looking into Hoglah's eyes, ignoring his visitor. "When I was awake before, I did not thank you." Hoglah waved away his words. "No, I must," he murmured, closing his eyes. "I was not always unconscious. Whenever my eyes opened you were there, cooling my forehead, smoothing my covers. Like an angel you hovered...."

Hanniel's arm fell limp from Hoglah's grasp as he retreated into deep sleep. Hoglah pushed some locks of his hair from his face. "Yes, sleep. You will need much of it to regain your strength."

Rizpah edged toward the door, eyeing the intimate scene. She left unnoticed.

Hanniel awoke to Hoglah's gentle nudging. She knelt at his side holding a steaming bowl of broth. He stared at her and she blushed. Her plainness had been softened in his eyes by her tender ministrations to him throughout his illness. Watching her stir the soup, he realized she was not so dull as he'd always thought. Only, compared to her sisters' shining beauty—well, she couldn't compare. *She has a beauty of her own that goes unnoticed,* thought Hanniel. *No wonder Ludim found so much to love in her.* His thoughts must have been reflected in his eyes, for Hoglah blushed deeper.

"Why do you stare?"

Why do I stare? Hanniel remembered Ludim's summation of Hoglah. After watching her reaction to her husband's death, Hanniel saw clearly how everyone had misinterpreted Hoglah's shyness and industry as strength. She had always held her emotions in check, not because she was strong, but because she couldn't face them. Studying her, he understood that were it not for the diversion of caring for him, she might have been undone by her grief. Ludim's dying request echoed in his ears, and his eyes clouded.

"Does your fever return?" Hoglah's brows came together as she reached to feel his face.

Hanniel jerked his head away, looking toward the wall. "No, no. I am only tired."

"Of course you are. You can sleep again after you've eaten."

"Many th-thanks to you, b-but I'm not hungry."

"But your broth. You need your stre—"

"M-maybe later."

Hanniel regretted the irration in his tone, but he could think of no other way out of the conversation. Reverberations of Ludim's pleas reached him from the depth of his delirium, where he thought he'd left them, like the echoes of a subterranean cave. Beneath the pleading was always the repetition of Rizpah's last rejection. Hanniel thrashed beneath his covers, wondering himself if he had returned to the feverish state that created these tauntings.

21

Rizpah urged her dragging feet onward. *Only a few hundred paces and we're home,* she promised them. For the past few days she had sneaked home while Tirzah slept during the burden and heat of the day, to steal some rest for herself.

Coming within view of Hoglah's tent, Rizpah saw Hanniel propped under the front tent flap. Hoglah fussed with his cushions. "Good day to you, sister," Hoglah hailed her as she neared the tent.

"And to you, Hoglah. I was on my way home to sleep, but you may need help subduing our active cousin."

"Help? Hanniel is such good company that I finish my chores before I know I've begun." She and Hanniel smiled at one another.

"I am so happy to see you recovered, Hanniel," Rizpah said, but to her surprise, instead of feeling pleased, she was irritated. "I was here a few days ago, but you had only just regained consciousness. You look well." Rizpah examined Hanniel's pale face and found his eyes bright and alert.

Hoglah gathered a basket of clothing in her arms and spoke before Hanniel could respond. "It is true that Hanniel is good company, but I *must* go to the river to wash our clothes, no matter how much I enjoy him. Good day." She started down the road, chatting with a woman she met on the way.

Hanniel looked at Rizpah's face as she watched her sister disappear. He studied each feature, awed that age had not dimmed her beauty. Her presence could brighten him so, yet also deepen his despair. The decision was now final. She had rejected him for the last time. He would ask Hoglah to marry him at the first opportunity. It must be as he had promised Elohim.

Rizpah turned to look at him, and he froze under her deep-golden gaze. "I am truly pleased at your quick recovery, but I must go now."

"No! I mean, please stay for a while. I'll be lonely if you leave."

"Well," she sighed, "I suppose you *shouldn't* be left alone so soon." She pulled a mat from the tent's interior and curled up on it.

"How is Tirzah?" he asked as he picked up a short reed and knife.

Rizpah smoothed her skirt. "The same. She's not laboring anymore, but I don't know how much longer we can hold the birth off. The longer she waits, the better she and the baby will fare."

Hanniel nodded. "I hear that Mahlah has married." He scraped the reed with the knife, shaping one end of it to a point.

"Oh, yes." Rizpah pulled at loose threads in her hem. "Nathan is wonderful for her. He appreciates her the way no one else could."

"No one but you."

"Well, I have always lived with Mahlah. I love her. It takes a man like Nathan to overlook her physical limitations to see that her value is limitless."

"I'm happy for her *and* Nathan." Hanniel paused and gouged at the reed. "I have seen Milcah. She helped to care for me. I think I have her to thank for my quick recovery."

"Yes, she is good with herbs."

"She seems different now." Hanniel blew the splinters from his gougings.

Rizpah rolled a twig between her fingers. "A little."

"Is it because of Othniel?"

Rizpah shrugged her shoulders, still avoiding his eyes. "I think I should go now. I need to rest before Tirzah wakes up and needs me."

Hanniel reached out and took hold of her arm. "What is wrong?" Rizpah turned her gaze upon him, bathing him with the dark amber of her soft eyes, and he was undone. "I m-mean, you s-seem so distant."

"Only tired."

"I am sorry. I am inconsiderate. You must need rest desperately."

"Well, not desperately." Her voice softened.

"I really would enjoy your company." He picked up the knife and reed again.

"What is that?" Rizpah relaxed on the mat.

"I'm making flutes for the girls. They have been so kind to give up their home and their mother so I could recuperate here—especially in the face of losing their father, may his soul rest in peace."

"May his soul rest in peace," Rizpah echoed. She paused. "Hoglah seems to be recovering from the shock of her husband's death quickly." Hanniel looked at her sharply. "I mean, she seems to be taking it well."

Hanniel was confused by the irritation in her voice. "I think she is not taking it as well as everyone believes. She will need the help of us all to endure this."

"Hoglah has never needed anyone's help."

"That's what I always thought, but I wonder if we have been wrong."

Anger sparked in Rizpah's eyes, but she blinked it away. Hanniel could not understand her attitude. Was she still upset that he had proposed again? He decided to let her know that she needn't worry about that any longer.

"Rizpah, I want to apologize for my actions on the night I returned."

"It is nothing."

"I have made a pest of myself for many years. If you can forgive me, it will never happen again."

A succession of relief, anger, and confusion flashed through Rizpah's eyes: not the reaction Hanniel had hoped for at all. "Did you hear me, Rizpah?"

She nodded.

"It will never happen again."

"I heard you." She jerked her head up and stared at him as if she confused even herself. "I mean, thank you. I mean, it is not necessary to talk of such things." She stared at the ground for a moment. "When will you return to the wars?"

"The campaigns have s-stopped until n-next spring. My leg should be healed by then."

"The soldiers who returned with you brought encouraging news."

" 'Encouraging' is not an apt description for what Elohim has wrought for His people. Rizpah, wherever we tread, there is victory." Hanniel's eyes shone and all traces of stuttering disappeared.

"That is not what I've heard of the battle against Ai."

"Not the first battle, but the fault was not with the Lord."

"So I've been told. Was the enemy's defeat sound the second time?"

"It could not have been sounder." Hanniel put aside the knife and reed flute, and Rizpah leaned forward to hear every detail of the conquest.

For over two hours they talked of war and of God's purpose for His people, and of the future. Hanniel was impressed with the wisdom Rizpah displayed in matters he thought were confined to men's interests. Still, he supposed, in a family where women had to fill both the male and female roles Rizpah's discernment should come as no surprise. Nevertheless, her many virtues astounded him.

"Are you still here?" Hoglah appeared, hauling her wet laundry.

Rizpah looked up and blinked. "Oh—I never meant to stay so long." She jumped up. "I have enjoyed our visit," she said, looking down at Hanniel. "I think we've never had the opportunity to sit and talk like this." She smiled.

"Thank you for giving up your rest for me."

"It was nothing." Rizpah flashed him another smile and hurried to attend to Tirzah.

Nothing, Hanniel's thoughts echoed, and he sighed.

22

Tirzah smiled at Rizpah from her bed, and her eyes crinkled. "I think I'll rest now." She stretched and yawned.

"It is still morning. You never sleep at this time."

"I never before knew who you spend time with while I rest."

"And what does that have to do with anything?"

"Nothing. It's just that I approve."

"Approve of what?"

Tirzah dropped her eyes.

"Approve of what, Tirzah? That I have found a friend?" Tirzah kept smiling. "We are only friends, Tirzah. He told me himself that he would never burden me with another proposal."

Tirzah looked surprised. "He did? I had thought that maybe..."

Rizpah was annoyed, but she hid her feelings well. "*I* thought that maybe you were too busy consoling this little one," she bent to pat her sister's swollen belly, "to be making a match."

Tirzah laughed. "You are right, but you may as well go with your friend Hanniel now, because I hear Mahlah coming to sit with me."

"Tirzah! You arranged everything, didn't you?"

"Well..." Tirzah was interrupted by the appearance of Mahlah, smiling happily as she was carried in.

Hanniel leaned against a sturdy oak, strumming his lyre. Ten days had passed since his fever broke, and he was so revived that today Rizpah took him to her secret place atop the mountain, overlooking the Yarmuk river. He was so well, in fact, that he now stayed at Mahlah and Nathan's home for propriety's sake, and Rizpah found she could relax more with him without the distraction of caring for Hoglah's girls.

Rizpah sat beside him, spinning with her hands. She pulled fibers from the wad of washed and combed wool tucked beneath her arm and twirled them between her fingers until she was satisfied with the bulk of the thread. Taking a break from the work, she leaned her head against the tree behind her and closed her eyes. *Why can't life always be like this?* she wondered.

Being with Hanniel was so peaceful, and peace was a feeling she had seldom experienced. She seemed to have always worried about whether Caleb would ever love her, or what the future would hold for their family of women. There had been her sickly mother to care for in her youth, who had grown so weak that Rizpah had prayed for death to hasten an end to her suffering. As she looked back on her life, she saw that she had wasted it looking forward, always waiting for something to happen. She'd always strained forward, the present being dead in her anticipation for the future. Now there was no future, but for the first time, she was enjoying the present.

I am forty years old. The number astonished her. How had so many years been eaten away in her pursuit of Caleb? She opened her eyes and watched Hanniel strum, his ruddy lips pursed with the expression he assumed when playing his lyre. Rizpah regretted that she had not befriended him years ago. She had always been so afraid that she would be forced to marry him, that she'd forfeited a precious friend.

Hanniel looked up at her and winked. "Would you like to play?"

At first Rizpah missed his meaning, her thoughts had been so distant. She looked at the lyre he held toward her. "I thought you let no one else play it."

"I don't, but for you, I'll make an exception—*if* you let me show you how to handle the instrument properly."

Hanniel moved closer, showing her how to cradle it in her lap and what to do with her hands. The sun showered them with warmth as the wind parted the upper leaves of the forest. Bright reflections glinted off the winding Yarmuk below them. She laughed as her awkward hands made twanging noises on the unfamiliar strings.

Hanniel handed her the plectrum. "Use this to sweep the strings—like this." He took her hand and strummed with it. "Make long, downward strokes. Now do this." He moved behind her and guided her left hand to put pressure on some of the strings, and with his right hand, started her strumming as he switched the pressure of her fingers on the upper strings at intervals, seducing the loveliest sounds from the lyre.

He repeated the procedure several times. "Now, try it alone." He sat back to watch her.

Rizpah began to play and was amazed at the results of her efforts. "Now, see there," Hanniel teased. "Soon you'll put my playing to shame."

Rizpah laughed. "Oh, yes, and before we know what's happened, I'll be hiring out to play at the feasts."

"Why, you brazen woman!"

Rizpah hesitated, but Hanniel's comment was obviously in jest, so she joined in his laughter.

"I'll teach you the words. Play the first chord four times." She did so, and Hanniel sang. "Now, change to the next chord," he instructed, and then continued singing. "Change to the next one," he stopped and said, but Rizpah fumbled before she found it. "Next chord. Next."

Rizpah laughed with the delight of making music. "Let's do it again. I had to concentrate so hard on what I was doing, I couldn't listen to the words."

"All right. This time, I'll point when it's time for you to change chords."

Rizpah nodded and situated her fingers for the first chord. Holding her other hand poised for strumming, she signaled she was ready. Hanniel sang as she played.

When the lily blooms
The flower covers its grave.
Much beauty hides much pain.
And much pain flowers
In the heart of a man who loves,
When the beauty buries his heart.

"What a tragic song! I've never heard it sung at the feasts."

"It's not a worship song. I wrote it."

Something in the tone of his grating voice told her the song was about her; *she* was the beauty that buried his heart. She stared at him. He stared back, and she knew intuitively from the softness that came over his dark eyes that he was going to kiss her. She didn't want him to, but curiosity about her own feelings silenced her. She longed to pull away, but she was spellbound, studying him like a priest poring over the beloved commandments of God.

Hanniel blinked, and his coarse voice strangled a whisper. "I will keep my word to you." He took the lyre from her hands and strummed, slowly at first. Then he burst into a familiar dancing tune. Relieved, Rizpah clapped to the music and sang with him, but the tragedy of his song lingered in her mind.

23

Hanniel was not at Mahlah's tent when Rizpah came for him. He was at Hoglah's, and at the word from her sister, Rizpah quickened her gait. She was late, and she looked forward to their midday visits so, she didn't want to waste any of the time today.

The breeze of the coming winter blew cool on her face. Rizpah looked to make sure no one was around to see her and then gave two short skips and a twirl and laughed at herself. How wonderful, to forget about lovers and problems and to concentrate on her growing friendship with Hanniel. What a fool she'd been not to know him sooner! How foolish to allow her obsession with Caleb control her life! Grabbing hold of Hoglah's door pole, she rounded the corner of the tent but stopped short at the sight before her.

Hoglah sat cross-legged on her embroidered rug. Hanniel knelt before her.

"You would do me great service if you would become my wife."

Hoglah blushed and looked into Hanniel's eyes for what seemed to Rizpah an eternity. Then she looked up and gasped. "Rizpah!"

Hanniel leaned back on his haunches and ran a stubby hand over his face. He rose and took a step toward her. "Rizpah, I didn't want you to find out like—"

Rizpah stepped defensively back. "And why not? Why would you want to hide such news? This is cause for celebration." Her voice caught.

The three looked from one to the other. Rizpah felt as if she'd been thrown from the cliffs of her secret place and was hurtling toward the rocks of the Yarmuk's banks. "Elohim's blessing on your union," she murmured and turned to leave.

"Come back," called Hanniel. Rizpah turned to face Hoglah, who opened her mouth soundlessly. And then anger flooded Rizpah completely, at the thought of Ludim, only two weeks dead.

"It is good you cannot speak, Hoglah. You would sin to make excuse for running so quickly to another's bed when your husband's is not yet cold."

"Rizpah!" Hanniel stepped to Hoglah's side and touched her hair, and Rizpah's hand involuntarily flew to her own. She trembled and turned on him.

"Have you turned from Elohim and His ways to commit such treachery to the memory of Ludim?"

"You cannot blame Hanniel. It is for Ludim that he—"

"Then should I blame you?" Rizpah's voice was scalding. "Do you intend to use Hanniel as a substitute for Ludim?"

Hoglah broke into sobs, as Hanniel crossed the tent in a bound and grasped Rizpah's shoulders roughly. "Never in my life have I been anything but proud of your actions, but this day you shame yourself. Look what you have done to your sister."

"What *I* have done to her?" Rizpah ripped her arms from his grip and straightened her garments, aghast at the tone of his voice. "Did I come into her tent and...and...did *I* seduce her from mourning her husband's death? You never even mourned him, Hoglah! Caleb was not taken from me in anything so final as death, and *I* mourned till I thought I would perish."

Hoglah gulped down her sobs. "Is that what you want of me? To see my misery? What a cruel person you are!"

"I only want to know that you have feelings like the rest of us."

"You see my tears—you hear my sobs." Hoglah thrust her streaked face forward. "Does it please you?"

Rizpah stepped back involuntarily, staring at her sister's outstretched hands in humiliation. She wanted to take them up and kiss them. Oh, how she longed to dry the tears that *she* had caused!

"Rizpah, why are you so angry at us?" Hanniel murmured.

"Rizpah!" Milcah's usually bright tone was heavy and her eyes narrowed. "Tirzah asks for you, Rizpah."

"I am sorry you had to come," Tirzah gasped.

Rizpah knelt beside her. "Don't be silly." Her words were terse with concern. "I shouldn't have left you alone."

"You have so little"—Tirzah held her breath for a pain—"time to yourself because of me," she finished.

"Shhh." Rizpah stroked Tirzah's forehead, smoothing back the matted hair. "Everything will be fine. Your little one is only insisting on some attention."

"Go find Reuben." Rizpah turned her head and bit the command into the air behind her, and Milcah, wide-eyed, rushed to carry out orders.

"Well," she turned back to her youngest sister. "Are you ready for this?" Tirzah held her stomach tightly and laughed. "Will you laugh your way through your first birthing?" Rizpah asked, her eyes softening with the tenderness she felt. She whispered, "Of us all, I think you are most like mother; so brave and gentle."

Tirzah gasped in the grip of another pain. Rizpah set herself to the job of coaxing her sister through a typical long first labor, but already Tirzah was straining forward, the veins in her neck popping as her head bowed up from the mat. Rizpah prayed for Elohim's protection desperately.

Hoglah burst into the tent. "Tirzah will need this later," she panted, placing her birthing stool beside their moaning sister. She gave Rizpah a long look, but her countenance was void of any anger.

"Are your girls alone?" Rizpah asked.

Hoglah shook her head. "Hanniel is with them."

Rizpah bit her lip as Hoglah bustled across the room to wet some strips of linen. Tirzah moaned and grasped the bed clothes in agony. "We may need the stool sooner than usual." Rizpah's brow furrowed.

Hoglah whirled toward her. "Do you mean—"

Tirzah doubled up and screamed. "It's going too fast," Rizpah said. "She shouldn't be—"

"Tirzah!" Reuben's scream matched his wife's as he appeared in the door. "I could hear her three tents away. Why is she screaming like that?" he demanded, angrily pushing the women aside and taking his wife in his arms.

"Get him out of here," Rizpah snapped.

"But you sent me for him," Milcah said.

"That was before she knew Tirzah's time was already upon her," Hoglah answered shortly.

Rizpah raised her eyebrows and examined Hoglah as Milcah dragged Reuben out of the tent, but another scream demanded her attention.

Exhausted, Rizpah flopped onto her own soft bed mat. She pulled her blanket tight to ward off the chill of the early autumn. A smile teased her tired lips in spite of her anger at Hoglah. Her arms could still feel the warmth of Tirzah's robust new son, the first male to be born into their family in two generations.

She was on the edge of sleep when she heard a deep male voice approaching the tent, followed by girlish giggling. The couple stopped outside. She heard the man imitate a marching command, stamping his feet in time, and a new burst of giggling erupted. This time Rizpah recognized Milcah's laugh, the same empty laugh she'd heard for months. Then silence—a long silence—and Milcah's hushed voice bid him good night.

When Milcah entered the center receiving section of the tent, Rizpah was in the doorway of her adjoining room. The faltering fire in the tent's center left her in shadow.

"Milcah." Milcah jumped and turned to see where Rizpah's voice had come from. "Do you think it wise to be out at night with a man?"

Milcah bent to fuel the fire and the flames lurched over her features. "It has never hurt before."

"You mean to say you do this often?"

"You have a comment to offer on everyone's life today, don't you?" Anger raised the pitch of Milcah's voice. "I'm surprised you trouble *me,* but I expected what you did to Hoglah. Everyone knows you've always disliked her."

"That is not true." Rizpah stepped foward. "How can you—"

"Oh, but it *is* true! You have never sought her friendship."

"That's not—not because I don't like her." Rizpah was breathless from shock. "I can't believe you think that."

"Then why have you ignored her all your life, if not because you hate her?"

"Hate her? The thought is ridiculous. I love my sisters—*all* of them. Only Hoglah never needed me the way the rest of you did. Hoglah never needed anyone—not even Ludim."

"Not even Ludim?" Milcah snorted. "I always thought you so wise, Rizpah, and now you say something so foolish. Can't you see? Only because of her great need of Ludim would she accept Hanniel's proposal. Otherwise, her grief may have killed her."

Rizpah fought the knowledge deep down that Milcah was right. "Grief didn't kill us," she spat bitterly.

"And you desire that Hoglah suffer as we have? Do you want her longing for soldiers in the moonlight to ease her pain? Should she retreat into some nowhere world as you did?"

"You know that's not what I mean."

"Then, what?"

Rizpah was silent. She was becoming confused. In Hoglah's tent she had seen everything so clearly—she had acted so righteously. She took a deep breath. "If Hoglah really loved Ludim, she could not even consider marrying someone else so soon."

"You mean that *you* could not think of loving someone else so soon after you lost *Caleb*." Milcah took a step toward her and Rizpah instinctively drew back. "At least you thought you couldn't, but you did love someone after Caleb."

"No, I—"

"Yes. You love Hanniel. Everyone can see it but you, and perhaps Hanniel. You won't admit it to yourself because you are so proud, Rizpah. You say you'd be abusing Caleb's memory. Well, Caleb is not dead, and you abuse his honor by making yourself a martyr in his name."

Rizpah was speechless, her head shaking back and forth numbly in denial.

"And what's worse, you drag Hanniel and Hoglah down with you. You won't have Hanniel so Hoglah cannot have him either." Milcah turned to leave, but her heart was softened. "Rizpah," she began softly. "I am sorry. You—I—"

Rizpah could hear no more. She stumbled out of the tent, breathless and dazed, her head still shaking in denial. *I don't love Hanniel. I don't!* The smack of cold air startled her; then she filled her lungs deeply and in determination, made her way to her secret place high in the hills.

She didn't remember stumbling over roots and fallen branches along the dark river path, or pushing past the thorny underbrush along the unused trail up to the highest cliff above the Yarmuk. She was conscious of nothing until she found herself balanced on a craggy overhang, protruding so far from the mountainside she felt as if she were suspended in midair. The frosty wind numbed her face and whipped at her robe until she felt again as if she were falling, hurtling once more into the deathly region where she'd lived her life: always waiting, always waiting for Elohim to grant her Caleb's love. Now, she had his love, even his admiration, but only as he gave it to men, to brothers. She felt tricked, but who had tricked her? Surely not Elohim.

Rizpah lifted her face to the sky, but there was only a sliver of moon, nothing to illuminate the return of her soul's deadness. For a time she'd climbed out of that region. When Caleb had asked her to marry him, she'd basked for the first time in the sunlight. Then, with one swoop, like the advance of the vulture, her uncle had persuaded Israel's God to cut off the sunlight. Why had Elohim done this to her? She could be Caleb's wife this minute. She *should* be! She'd earned the right. She'd given up everything most women hold dear for the privilege of marrying Caleb, and she had come so close. What had gone wrong?

Rizpah's mind returned to that dreadful time of rejection, to the time when everything she had lived for was crushed. Once more she relived the time darkness overtook her soul; and she welcomed it, for it had cushioned her then, protecting her from her own grief. But this time, it was different.

Elohim removed the protective barriers she'd erected around her heart and the pain of loss burned in her stronger than it ever had been allowed to before. Rizpah's head lolled, and her eyes poured out agony with tears such as she'd never shed. The tears scorched her face and neck and set the yoke of her robe aflame.

She thought she would be consumed with wanting Caleb; but no, she did not desire Caleb anymore; only to be released from this prison she'd built, only to return to the kiss...that kiss....*No! I don't love Hanniel!* Still she burned, until her spirit and soul were seared apart. Unable to contain her struggle any longer, Rizpah threw back her head, her spine arched like a drawn bow, and she raised her arms to Elohim.

"Help me, please!" she screamed into the darkness. "Lord God of Israel, I can take this no longer. Help me!"

The next she knew, she lifted her head from the ground, her hair and robe wet with dew, and the sun was sending tentative probes into the purple sky. Rizpah recalled the torture of her last consciousness, realizing she was not crumpled on the barren rocks of the precipice. She was curled into the protective hollow of an old willow, nestled in the furry grass, her robe secured around her for warmth.

She remembered she had awakened in the night with a peace that jarred her, with the silence of a presence in the night, and she was free—free from the tension, the turmoil, the struggling. All her life, Rizpah had sensed a destiny. It warmed her in her youth, drove her in young adulthood, and burned within her in middle age. Last night when she had awakened, the truth was all so clear. She had a destiny, yes, but she had staked the tent pegs of pursuit in the wrong place: in Caleb. As she had settled beneath the towering willow last night, she broke camp and made her exodus from always waiting. She took up residence beneath the shadow of Elohim's love, in the region that was rightfully hers.

The sound of voices drifted to her and she scrambled to a sitting position. She pulled her robe tightly around her and squinted in the direction of the sound. She heard footsteps, and Hanniel stepped out of the forest. Their eyes met and Rizpah's heart leapt. She felt light and warmth within her, not the scorching desire of yearning. Agony and death were replaced with cleansing light, like that which tumbled over the eastern hilltops. *I love him!*

And then Hoglah stepped beside Hanniel. Rizpah stared mutely. They were paired so beautifully.

"I told you she would be here," Hanniel said to Hoglah, and they walked toward her.

24

Hoglah helped Rizpah lie back on her mat once more. She turned to Hanniel and shooed him out. "She needs rest now. We can talk later."

Rizpah moaned, exhausted, as Hanniel left. Her heart was now heavy. After causing Hanniel so much pain for so many years she could not interfere with his happiness. She must sacrifice the man God had saved for her, because she hadn't recognized him. Her heart had been caught up with Caleb, the mighty man of God, the courageous soldier, the valiant general, the deliverer. Her sight had been shaded by glory, and she had overlooked the meek, the steadfast, the faithful. Hanniel's very virtues had been her stumbling block, and now she had lost him. There was no redemption to be found.

"Hoglah," she grunted, raising herself to a sitting position.

"Oh, no." Hoglah put her hands on Rizpah's shoulders. "You lie down and rest."

"No. I need to talk to you." Their eyes met, and Hoglah, seeing Rizpah's resolve, nodded and removed her hands. "Please, sit with me." Hoglah settled herself obediently.

"What I did to you yesterday was unforgivable." Hoglah was silent, staring at her hands folded neatly in her lap. "I know that it was in caring for Hanniel that you snapped out of an unbearable grief. I know you loved Ludim terribly. I don't know why I said all those things. I guess I was just..." Her voice trailed off.

"You were jealous, Rizpah." Hoglah's tone was soft, but Rizpah's eyes narrowed, studying her closely. "Don't be angry with the truth."

Rizpah sighed. "I'm not angry anymore, Hoglah. I was selfish to destroy your moment of happiness. Will you forgive me?"

Slowly Hoglah reached over to clasp Rizpah's hand. At her touch, Rizpah's defenses tumbled and instantly two sisters were in each other's arms, weeping.

"Be happy with him," Rizpah sniffed. "He's a good man."

Hoglah pulled away. "Why is it that Hanniel is the only one who *asked* me if I would marry him? Everyone else *tells* me I will."

Rizpah was stunned. *Could it be? Could Hoglah have declined his proposal?*

Hoglah smiled. "I do not love him in that way, Rizpah. No one could take Ludim's place—not now."

Rizpah barely heard Hoglah's explanation of Hanniel's promise, of his heroic attempt to save Ludim's life. She had been lifted into the sunlight of the new day. She had to find Hanniel.

But Hanniel was not to be found. No one had seen him since his return from the mountain, and everyone had noted with concern the despair that clouded his face. Rizpah was also beginning to fear, and then she knew.

Hanniel strummed his lyre and stared, sightless, from the cliffs where Rizpah came to pour out her most secret feelings. Sitting where he had found her this morning, he could almost feel her presence. *What does she dream of here?* he mused. He closed his eyes and strummed.

He must leave. Hoglah would not marry him, and he'd caused Rizpah enough grief. With all she had suffered these last years, his presence could only cause her more pain.

The sunlight warmed his face, but his numb fingers hardly felt the strings they swept in the melancholy tune he'd taught Rizpah. His mind flittered over his memories of her. Never again could he draw from her great strength, or watch her work in that sure, quick way she had about her, or simply bask in her smile. And with these thoughts, the sun ceased to warm even his face.

"Hanniel?"

Hanniel opened his eyes. Rizpah stood over him. *Is she only my memory?* But she called his name again. He scrambled to his feet. "Rizpah! What are you—" He halted as he took in her appearance. Her eyes sparkled within the dust-smeared circle of face. She had not washed since her night on the mountain, and her hair tumbled freely about her shoulders. Her damp, wrinkled robe still smelled of grass and night air, but to him she looked like an angel, in all its glory.

He couldn't help himself. He reached out to wipe a smudge from her cheek. She didn't flinch from his touch. Puzzled, he dropped his hand, peering into the golden pools of her eyes. Again he touched her cheek. She only gazed at him, open to him for the first time. He cupped her chin and their eyes locked.

"Marry me, Hanniel."

He stared. Had she spoken? Was he dreaming?

"Marry me." Her voice was insistent.

And then the sun warmed him again—enveloped him in its rapture. He crushed Rizpah to him, kissing her tangled hair, her temples, her cheeks, her lips. Their kiss mingled with the cries of the birds that fluttered from the treetops.

"Marry me, Hanniel," Rizpah commanded against his lips.

Hanniel drew back and smiled at her, his voice nearly lost in her desperate gaze. He managed to croak his compliance.

"Why, you brazen woman!"

The cliffs threw back the sound of their laughter for them to savor again and again, as if in compensation for the empty years behind them.